MAKING THE BEST
OF THE
ZOMBIE APOCALYPSE

A Novella

Alisha Adkins

Copyright 1999, 2012 by Alisha Adkins
ISBN-13: 978-0615680750 (Rhapsody in Lime Publishing)
ISBN-10: 0615680755

Cover and Interior Formatting: Streetlight Graphics

To my mother.

Table of Contents

Chapter 1 - Keeping Mother 3

Chapter 2 - Survivors of the Apocalypse 17

Chapter 3 - Perfect Storm 29

Chapter 4 - Nothing Left to Lose 43

Chapter 5 - Unburdened 61

Chapter 6 - Mother's Milk 77

Chapter 7 - The Winds of Change 89

Chapter 8 - Another One Bites... 101

Chapter 9 - Letting Mother Go 113

Chapter 10 - So It Goes 119

Chapter 11 - Meeting Adjourned 123

Chapter 12 - Things Could Be Worse 141

Excerpt from Flesh Eaters 153

Excerpt from Daydreams of Seppuku 167

Excerpt from Death: the Travelogues 173

About the Author 177

Scavenged from the rubble, these two personal accounts have been edited and compiled together as part of an ongoing attempt to preserve the post-apocalyptic history of the living.

Chapter 1 - Keeping Mother

I have kept my mother chained to the frame of her bed for a little over two years now. I don't even really hear the racket she makes anymore. The scraping of her chains against the metal frame, her moaning, and the spluttering, guttural noises—they're all just background sounds now, as natural as the chirping of birds or the hum of crickets.

How long should we hold onto our zombie children or zombie mothers out of sentimentality, a sense of duty, or unwillingness to accept change? Behavioral scientists could undoubtedly make good research of this question, if they weren't all busy studying zombies or being zombies themselves these days.

I know it's not my mother anymore. It's just the flesh that my mother used to inhabit.

Soulless, hungry flesh. To be honest, it doesn't really even look much like my mother anymore.

And I know that keeping her can only serve to do me harm—living with a corpse inevitably produces unhygienic living conditions and promotes an unhealthy mental state. On top of that, there is a certain level of stress that is unavoidable when you live with the knowledge that something that wants to eat you is never more than a room or two away. And that's not to mention the very real and ever present danger that she may eventually succeed...

Still, letting her go is unthinkable.

I mean, what can I do? She's my mother.

After my divorce, I moved in with my mother. She was getting on in years, and I was worried about her being all alone in her house in the suburbs. I did it for her sake, but her companionship helped ease my own loneliness as well. I'd gone from living in a house teeming with life—a wife, two young children and a dog—to living in a chillingly silent, unnaturally still apartment literally overnight. My wife had full custody, and I found myself working longer and longer hours just so I didn't have to face the emptiness of my new "home." So, if I'm really honest with myself, moving in with Mother benefited us both. Even if she was just puttering around in another room, I found the sounds of her presence comforting. In some ways, I guess I still do.

Mother and I lived together about three years before the End of Days, as my mother called it, and about another year after the zombies came. "Nathan," she used to say—my name is Nathan, by the way—"Nathan, it's the end time now. Judgment Day is upon us." She never quite worked out why judgment never came or, if it had, why *everyone* had apparently been condemned to suffer.

Now I still live with Mother, but she no longer lives at all.

Some days, I don't even go into her room. It's easier when I don't have to look at her. On those days, I can just go about my daily routine. Everything is normal, and the scratching, rustling, and moaning are just vague reminders of having some companionship within the house. I tell myself that Mother is just a little sick right now, that's all.

Zombies don't actually get colds, of course, though I did once think that Mother must be coming down with the sniffles when her nose started to run. It turned out to just be her brain liquefying.

Sometimes I feel as though I'm a terrible son. I mean, I keep my mother chained by her hands and feet to the bed. And I don't really feed her. Under the circumstances, I think I've done the best I could, but it still certainly sounds callous if you put it down in words.

Other than a few rats that I've trapped, Mother hasn't eaten in two years. So, I'm sure that Mother is extremely hungry. The problem is that she won't eat anything that isn't alive. When I first restrained her in her bedroom and began my "hospice" care, I tried to feed her soup. That was a disaster. Then, for my next attempt at feeding her, I tried giving her scraps of humans and animals that I had scavenged, but she still showed not even the faintest interest. Flesh is apparently uninteresting to her if it doesn't still retain the warmth of life. The only meal she consistently expresses desire for is me.

Today, I knew I had to tidy up in her room. I'd put it off for far too long.

As soon as I open the door, the heavy wave of stench hits me.

One step back, deliberately exhale, and then, back rigid, I enter. I have ritualized this task by now. Somehow, it makes it easier.

One quick burst of Lysol to try to dilute the air. I'd like to spray more, but it has to be conserved.

Flies buzz against the windows. If Mother could reach them, perhaps they would provide a snack. I swat them with a rolled up newspaper. The sheer, once yellow, curtains are tattered and stained. I brush off the crushed flies that have adhered to the fabric. I'll sweep them up before I leave.

Using a bucket and sponge, I attempt (rather

futilely) to remove the gunk and splatters that have most recently accumulated upon the walls. This is my routine.

Once I have run out of other tasks in the room, I finally turn to Mother.

She is straining against her chains, leaning as far forward on the bed as the shackles will allow.

Though it was at great personal risk to myself, I used to try to wipe down my mother. After all, in order to respect her memory, I felt that her body deserved to be maintained with some level of dignity. However, after I realized that the rag I used to wipe off her ooze and muck was also coming away with skin and the occasional bone fragment, I gave up on the practice.

So, if I allow myself to be honest about it, Mother looks pretty damned bad.

I try not to examine her features, but some things I still can't avoid noticing. Lately, I've begun to think that her jaw is coming loose. Not that there is anything I can do about that.

Mother wears an old house dress. If I remember correctly, it used to be blue. It's hardly more than a filth-soaked rag now that loosely drapes her withered frame. I would try to change her clothes, but there is just no way to adequately subdue her.

My mother has worn that dress since the day she passed. I guess, in some small way, I have a grown a sentimental attachment to it over the years.

Unfortunately, after she was bitten, Mother did not die right away.

After the End Time began, I saw that my mother never left the safety of the house. I took care of all of the supply gathering and our other needs. She was in her sixties, after all. I was the good, dutiful, protective son I should have been. I continue to remind myself of this, to console myself with this.

Mother was infected by a young woman that she innocently let into our home. While I was away on a supply run, a woman of about twenty had come to our door. She made a great deal of noise, pleading to be let in.

⌒◦◦◦⌒

"I heard someone moving around in there. And I saw light from your window. Please, I know there's someone alive in there. There are zombies out here—I'm scared. Please, please let me in!"

Mother was a softy. She let the girl in, fed her, and comforted her, listening to the girl's story. One thing about End Time—everyone has a story to tell.

I think Mother thought that I needed a girlfriend. But she didn't realize that this girl could not make a suitable mate. She had been bitten, though she concealed it from both of us.

When I returned home that evening, I was exasperated with Mother for letting her inside our house. The girl could have been part of a group that was laying in wait out of sight to swarm our residence and claim it for themselves. Anything could have happened, really. I privately scolded her for not being careful enough.

"Please be more careful, Mother! You're all I have. What if something happened to you? Please don't put yourself in danger."

My mother had just smiled and patted my arm.

It did seem like we'd dodged a bullet, though. The girl was nice, and kind of cute besides. We ate dinner together (some cans of beans I had found in an abandoned house earlier that day), chatted affably, and then Mother put out pillows and a quilt for the girl to sleep on our sofa.

The girl died quietly while lying on our sofa that night. She returned less quietly—Mother, always a light sleeper, heard her knocking about and bumping into things—and went to see what was happening (she was probably worried that one of her collection of glass figurines would be broken in the ruckus).

The girl—or former girl, or whatever I should call her—attacked my mother, taking a hefty bite out of her forearm before I was able to run into the living room and peel her off of my mother.

I smashed that bitch corpse's skull in with one of Mother's heavier crystal figurines—a blue jay, I think it was—that still sat intact upon the end table. I kept hitting until there was just a pile of muck where her head should have been.

But why do I play this over yet again in

my mind? It's old news, and nothing can be changed now. After being bitten, Mother suffered through terrible pain for several days before she succumbed to the infection and died. I had the foresight to restrain her. Now we live together in a different way.

There's something horrifying about the notion of seeing something you love corrupted and defiled. But, if you see it often enough, you get used to it. It becomes the new normal. As upsetting as it is to live with the zombified remains of my mother, I can't imagine how I'd fill my days now without her... Looking after Mother, and keeping our environment relatively sanitary in spite of her, gives me purpose and provides a daily routine. And, as tragic as it may be, when I look into the vacant sockets that once contained her eyes, memories of my boyhood still flood back to me.

Sitting slightly forward and staring blankly into the depths of those sockets as I sat next to Mother's bed in the bergére chair that she had so lovingly and painstakingly reupholstered nearly a decade ago, when my ex-wife, Becky, was pregnant with our first child, I guess that I got lost in my thoughts. Before I realized what was happening, Mother lunged for me, grazing my cheek with her desiccated lips. A millimeter closer and her teeth would have made contact before I was able to draw back.

I gasped as I pulled back from her with such sudden force that I practically tipped my chair over backwards. Adrenaline rushing and heart pounding in my ears, I unconsciously pushed the chair away with my long legs, finding myself already a good three feet away before I was even conscious of what I was doing.

My zombie mother's head was still thrust forward, matted clumps of her unkempt hair falling over her face, mercifully obscuring her misshapen features, although I could still make out her teeth fiercely gnashing.

I sat very still and let my heart slowly return to its normal pace.

She—it—was still occasionally jerking against her chains, though I think she sensed that her opportunity had passed. Her motions lacked their previous fervor, as though she had resigned herself to the fact that, at least for the time being, her efforts were destined to be fruitless.

After about five minutes, I was breathing normally and my heart had grown quiet again. I looked at the book on the end table which now sat between the bed and the chair in which I sat. It was a book I had read many times. Unfortunately, I had left most of my library in storage after my divorce, and Mother's collection had been limited, especially once you sifted out the books on needlepoint and positive affirmations. Since I was essentially a shut-in by necessity, and there was no electricity for television or Internet, reading at the window was my primary diversion. I generally liked to spend a few hours reading at Mother's bedside, just for the company our presences might afford one another. Today, since Mother had almost eaten me, I decided to forgo it.

Letting out a sigh, I got up, returned the chair to its standard position in the room, mumbled my usual goodbye to Mother with less conviction than usual, and left the room, locking the door behind me.

Chapter 2 - Survivors of the Apocalypse

We meet once a month. We're a support group, I suppose. Survivors of the Apocalypse. It seems laughable and absurd that one of the few vestiges of our former society that has endured is the creation of self-help groups, but it does serve a function of sorts. You would think that it wouldn't be worth leaving the safety of our hideaways, braving numerous dangers, facing death many times over in order to have a cup of instant coffee and spend a couple of hours with strangers. But you'd be surprised how far up the ladder social interaction climbs in one's hierarchy of needs when you don't have it for a month at a time.

Besides, if you skip a month, all the other survivors presume you've died, so there's kind of a sense of obligation to keep the appointment.

One of the most difficult aspects of maintaining membership in our "club" is simply keeping track of the days. I mark mine off each morning when I see the first rays of sunlight. Otherwise I would have no accurate sense of time anymore.

So what is so compelling about our meetings? What drives us to keep this monthly appointment, tracking the days until our next meeting with people that we don't even really know? I frequently find myself shaking my head and asking myself that question—but I'm looking forward to going to the next one nonetheless.

When we meet, we really just talk. We share our stories of how we first became aware of the outbreak, of our previous lives, of our current existences, and, if we can bear it, of those we have lost along the way. It's a place to vent and to feel insulated from the world—to feel safe for a couple of hours. I guess that's the real appeal.

Honestly, I am not completely sure how our little organization came into being. My knowledge is limited and lacks pertinent details; you see, I am just a Johnny-come-lately, not one of the founders. Unfortunately, none of the original members are still with us, so some of the lore associated with the group has already been lost. Keeping accurate historical records is proving to be a very difficult task in our post-apocalyptic world.

I can only speak authoritatively about what I have personally experienced, which provides an incomplete record of the activities of the group over the last year. Nonetheless, an incomplete record is better than no record at all; in a civilization that is historically bereft, I figure that beggars cannot be choosers. Any history, even if flawed, is better than none.

I first stumbled upon the Survivors almost a year ago while I was out scavenging for food and cleaning supplies.

Foraging is a stressful activity. All of the

stores were looted years ago, so the only way to still find goods in a city is by going door to door between houses or apartments in a complex. This is a hit or miss proposition - often the residence to which I gain entry has already been picked over, and if it hasn't, there is frequently a former tenant to dispatch. With all the mayhem of the apocalypse, it surprises me how many people actually died in their homes, seemingly of starvation. I'd say a good third of the population must have found a place to hide after End Time came. Most of those people seem to have chosen to die quietly of starvation in their homes instead of facing the zombies milling around outside of their doors. So much for mankind's will to survive. It's certainly a more peaceful end than being ripped apart by zombies, I must admit. And I guess there's some dignity in that. The poor things don't retain much of that dignity in death though—they shuffle aimlessly around their apartments, their constant pacing wearing away the carpet beneath their feet.

In zombie movies, people are always surprised by a zombie lurking in a dark corner somewhere. That's such bullshit. You can generally tell if a zombie is in a house as soon as you jimmy open the door. The stench is the biggest cue, but even if your olfactory senses were impaired, all you would need to do is look down. If a zombie has been cooped up in the same place for any length of time, their repetitive movement will have etched patterns into the floor. Zombies are restless. Unless their limbs are impaired, the damned things are constantly walking; they don't stand still for very long and they never sit down.

I had just entered my fourth apartment of the day. There were no signs of the dead there, and its residents had left a few items of interest behind in their kitchen cabinets. I was rejoicing in the discovery of two boxes of stale macaroni that were infested with weevils. In my previous life, I would have dropped them into the trash in disgust. Now I was just grateful for the added protein.

There was a window in the kitchen. From it, I saw a flicker of motion out of the corner of my eye.

Plastering my back to the wall to make sure that I would not be seen, I peered out of the window. A man—a living man—was putting something on a telephone pole across the street. And then he was gone.

Quickly tossing the boxes of macaroni and some bars of soap that I had found in the apartment into my backpack, I left the residence and headed out to the point across the street where the man had been.

By the time I reached the spot where he had been, there was no sign of him. However, what he had placed on the telephone pole turned out to be a flyer.

"Survivors of the Apocalypse—you are not alone. The living unite - next meeting will be held in the Carrollton library on May 12th at noon. Refreshments will be served."

The group recruits by posting messages around the city—in case others are out there—listing the time of the next meeting. Their success has been quite limited. This is probably because there are so few living remaining to find their posts and those who do survive probably are still alive because they avoid going out as much as possible. At any rate, only a few recruits have been obtained through this method of advertising, but the group is still dedicated to trying to find more living to add to its ranks. They place make-shift flyers on phone poles, the sides of buildings, adhered to windows, plastered across surviving street signs, any available space.

I really wasn't sure if I should, but curiosity got the best of me, so I went.

That first meeting that I attended consisted of me and five other people. Initially, when I first arrived, I discovered that I felt quite awkward around strangers. Although this had never been the case for me in the past, this was my first social encounter since the zombie outbreak, and I had no idea what were appropriate social mores anymore. I was nervous, uncomfortable, and strongly regretting that I had come. Viewing myself from the perspective of an outsider for the first time since the world had changed, I was suddenly overcome with an overwhelming sense of shame over how I had been conducting my life. I didn't dare admit to anyone that I shared my home with Mother in her necrotic condition or that I had eaten human meat out of desperation on a couple of occasions.

Fortunately, nobody put me on the spot. Everyone mingled, got a cup of instant coffee, and then we pulled our chairs into a loose circle and people shared voluntarily. I quickly realized as I listened to other members speaking frankly about their raw, emotional, and ugly experiences, that the way I was conducting my life wasn't far from the norm. Or maybe, more accurately, there were no norms anymore. My actions didn't fall into the category of taboo though, and that was a huge relief.

I did little more than introduce myself at that first meeting, but everyone seemed satisfied with just my presence. Then we ate some stale Little Debbies snack cakes (rare and highly prized spoils that would fetch a hefty price in trade on the black market), savored the comfort and safety we felt together, and then looted some books before we departed.

One meeting and I was hooked.

For the first two meetings I attended, I walked to our designated meeting place. However, now I just drive a Hummer. I acquired it a little over a year ago. Gasoline is extremely scarce and the hum of an engine generally attracts the attention of any zombies in the vicinity, so I use it very sparingly. However, it has become my preferred means of transportation for our monthly meetings, especially if the weather is looking iffy. Being caught out on foot in the midst of a storm is not desirable—especially because inclement weather reduces visibility and drowns out the sound of approaching mobs.

Survivors of the Apocalypse definitely has advantages. And, as nice as companionship and even a fleeting sense of safety are, those aren't the only functions it serves. In a world stripped of the Internet, apps, cell phones, television, and even newspapers, I must admit, I had been starving for information. Although limited, I am extremely grateful for the knowledge that membership in the group has provided.

For instance, I've learned that a fair number of people keep zombies like I do, generally because it's just too hard to let go. People tenderly hold on to their parents, their spouses, their children. I think keeping children must be especially hard. For instance, Maggie, a petite, sweet-looking older lady in our group who looks as though she probably went to church every Sunday of her life, keeps her former grandchild locked in its "playroom." I try not to picture the life she goes home to after our meetings.

Although nobody in Survivors has admitted to doing it themselves, a couple of fairly reliable sources have recounted tales of other men keeping zombies for less sentimental, more unseemly, reasons. Apparently they knock out their teeth and use them as sex slaves—even trick them out for supplies. I personally can't understand that. I can't imagine why anyone would want to get off in a rancid, putrefying orifice. One's own hand is lot warmer, not to mention more hygienic.

As for cannibalism, it seemed that survivors

had independently all pretty much come to the same conclusion. It was a necessary evil. The critical shortage of meat began almost immediately after zombies began to appear. Within a few weeks, all supermarket meat had either been looted or had spoiled in its cases. Canned meat and other protein dense foods like legumes were quickly scavenged. In all but the most rural of areas in the United States, there was almost a complete lack of livestock , so the living were rapidly growing alarmed by their limited diets. Meals consisting entirely of dry cereal, potato chips, or even breath mints rapidly became the norm, and such nutrient poor eating habits led to weakness, slowed reflexes, and increased likelihood of being overcome by the dead. So cannibalism had soon become an accepted practice.

And, as we all quickly learned, eating a zombie doesn't turn you into one. Eating the flesh of the recently deceased, whether they have reanimated as zombies or not, doesn't cause the infection. The most serious concern associated with consuming human corpses is merely the levels of bacteria that may be present. The fresher the meat, the better. If you eat something that has had too much time to decay, the resulting stomach cramps can be sheer agony.

Chapter 3 - Perfect Storm

This month, when I arrived, I discovered that a new member had joined the group—a woman named Tempest.

"Is that her name or her tag?" I wondered to myself.

Post-apocalypse, many people reinvented themselves, adopting new names akin to gamer tags to accompany their new identities. Since the End of Days, people were no longer the same people they had been. Husbands and wives, mothers and fathers, lawyers, accountants, gas station attendants—these labels lost pertinence and were rarely retained. What people had been in their previous lives was irrelevant and painful to remember. Many survivors shed their pasts completely, including the birth names associated with them.

Tempest was hot as hell. She was all long, wild and disheveled blonde hair and green eyes adorned with smudged black eyeliner. She was also obviously damaged goods though, even by post-apocalyptic standards. The exterior she presented was as tough as nails, and if there was a soft interior lurking anywhere beneath her surface, it appeared likely to remain safe behind her impenetrable diamond-hard exterior for the indefinite future. If she had a soft and gentle side, an ounce of vulnerability, it was anybody's guess as to what might be an effective means of accessing it. She was undeniably sexy in her torn jeans, clingy tank top, and black leather jacket—cool, aloof, and impermeable.

I tried not to notice, but I really could not help but watch her as she strode around the room introducing herself to other members of the group. I was eager to learn her story.

❧

Besides Tempest, all the standard people were in attendance: Maggie, Dave, Gabe, Ron, and Tex.

Maggie is a rather doddering woman in her fifties who always arrived clothed in house dresses and sensible shoes. Not that I am casting aspersions regarding Maggie's fashion sense. There isn't a lot of incentive for dressing up under our current circumstances; I can't imagine that she has much of anyone to impress. Besides, donning glamorous attire that limits maneuverability, such as evening gowns and stiletto heels, would be not only socially inappropriate, but an outright detriment to survival. Still, as terrible as I feel about making the association, I can't help thinking of Monty Python's pepper pot ladies every time I see her.

Dave is the historian of the group. God only knows what he did before the apocalypse, but he is the keeper and compiler of knowledge now. He is probably only in his late forties, but his appearance is slipshod and ramshackle, with a wide, nasty scar that runs like a fissure through the right side of his face. Although Dave is missing an eye, he unfortunately only sometimes seems to remember to wear a patch over it. The patch does nothing to improve his condition, of course, but is entirely for the benefit of those around him.

Gabe is a younger man, in his early thirties at most, with a large, muscular physique. He joined only a few months ago and is still warming up to the group. He has made allusions to losing someone close to him—I think he may have said it was his wife—but he hasn't opened up and told his full story yet. The group doesn't push. We're happy to have our members even if they choose to permanently remain quiet.

And then there's Ron and Tex. Ron is small and wiry, in his early fifties, and always seems to be wearing a grimy baseball cap. Tex is his dog. Ron consistently comes to the meetings accompanied by Tex.

Tex's features are so mangled that it was impossible to tell what breed of dog he is. He is missing an eye and half an ear, and his body is crisscrossed with scar tissue. The dog's fur apparently won't grow over scars, so the poor animal's coat is so sparse that it looks like Tex has mange.

Tex has saved Ron's life more times than Ron can count.

Dogs are highly sought after companions

these days. In fact, I've heard that they trade for massive amounts of supplies on the black market. And it's no wonder. Dogs have proven to be immune to zombie infection. And, because of their keen senses of smell, they hate zombies to begin with—they recognize when something is dead, and they know that dead things should not get up and walk around. A dog is going to distrust anything ambulatory that smells like *that*. Now toss in a canine's protective nature, and any hostile action a zombie might begin to take toward a dog's master is going to immediately have that dog worked into a zombie-loathing attack frenzy.

Unless specifically trained, a dog will not know that it should take out the head, but any dog still can certainly slow a zombie down a hell of a lot.

I have heard Ron tell the tale of his first zombie encounter at almost every one of our meetings.

A few days after the "infection" was first reported, back when there was still television programming to report things, Ron was attacked by a zombie for the first time.

Ron was entering his fifties, divorced, owned

a modest home, and loved his dog. Like most people, he had been following the reports of the strange infection with some concern, but he was still going about his daily life. He got up and went to work at the auto shop, stopped for beer and cigarettes, then came home and fixed himself something simple for supper. Ron had run into a couple of people who said they had seen someone infected, but he hadn't come face to face with one himself.

Then one morning, Ron was getting ready to leave for work when Tex started making a huge commotion, barking, growling, and scratching at the front door.

Ron couldn't shut him up, so he let him out. He reasoned that maybe the poor dog had diarrhea.

Leaving the house to go to work, Ron exited the house, locked the front door, and began speaking to Tex without even looking around.

"Tex, you're going to have to stay out while I'm at work, you crazy dog. I can't have you shitting all over the house. Tex?"

Turning around, Ron saw that Tex was poised to attack a man who was approaching the house.

"Tex! No! Come here!" Ron had shouted frantically, trying to keep his dog from doing something horrible that would get him taken away and put down.

Oddly, the man was ignoring the menacing dog that was glaring at him and growling ferociously through its bared teeth.

More oddly still, the man looked like he'd already been attacked by something. He had an unhealthy greenish pallor and several visible wounds that looked infected...

"Infected..." That word seemed to bounce around inside Ron's brain for a moment, and then he said "oh, shit" under his breath.

At that moment, as the man continued to amble toward Ron who was standing at the front door, Tex sprung.

As Ron had proudly recounted to every living person he had encountered since, "Tex grabbed that zombie's leg, gnashing and tearing, and had pulled him back, away from me by several yards, before I even realized what was happening. Then he managed to bite through a tendon or something. He rendered that poor fucker's leg pretty much useless, and that zombie went down

35

like a sack of bricks."

At that point, the zombie, now crawling toward Ron while being bitten in the ass by a large, angry dog, was substantially less of a threat than it had been a few short moments before when it was still able to walk erect and was not yet encumbered by an enraged canine.

Ron had turned around and unlocked the door, got his shotgun, and dispatched his would-be assailant. Then he and Tex went back in the house. Ron called in sick to work that morning. The next morning, out of courtesy, he tried to call in again, but nobody ever answered there again.

Our meetings traditionally begin with a moment of silence in honor of the former members of our little club who are no longer with us. We don't know what has happened to any of them for sure, but in general terms, we can pretty much guess.

We all bowed our heads. Afterwards, as is customary, Dave opened the meeting with a general welcome and cursory overview of the agenda. The floor was then opened up to give each person a chance to speak.

❦

It took a little while, but by my third meeting, I was comfortable enough to open up and was ready to start to unburden myself. Since then, I've recounted my tale whenever the group acquires a new member, which admittedly doesn't happen all that often. Today was the third time I have told my story.

I've promised myself that I'll be thorough here. To be honest, whether this account is exhaustive or even accurate is largely inconsequential; it's only real importance is to me, but if I can't maintain my own internal code, what is left? My experiences during that time were not particularly unusual or uncommon, but they are mine, so I will share here at least a rudimentary summary of how I first came to discover that hell had come to earth.

❦

I was driving on the highway in my Honda Accord when I first became aware of the dawn of Zombie Era. Traffic seemed to be piling up ahead; I was heading toward some sort of slow down.

As I slowed to a crawl behind the cars in front of me, I saw that, perhaps a dozen car lengths ahead of me, there were several cars stopped at askew angles. At first I thought it was a regular accident.

But there was an awful lot of commotion... People were out on the road, and it looked like there must be injuries. I slowed to a stop some distance from the pile up because I suspected I might need to try to turn around, drive on the shoulder, or perform some other not-strictly-legal vehicular maneuver to get around the mess. You can imagine my dismay as I realized that two of the motorists ahead of me had exited their cars, walked over to a third motorist, and began eating his face. What should I do? Try to stop these lunatics? While still debating, more ravenous motorists with a myriad of alarming injuries began to display similar behavior. A few cars had already pulled to a stop behind me. I made a spur of the moment decision, peeled out, performed a three-point turn, and got the hell out of dodge. Turning on the radio, I soon learned that what I had witnessed was not an isolated incident. I won't go into details, but I performed some damned unusual driving that day as I raced home to safely wall up myself and Mother.

After I finished sharing my story, Dave took the floor. As soon as he had begun to speak, I stole a glance at Tempest. She had taken off her jacket, and she was even more shapely than I had previously thought. I also caught a glimpse of a tattoo on her upper arm, but I couldn't quite make out what it was.

After I had taken her in for as long as I could comfortably get away with, I reluctantly turned my attention to Dave.

Dave is the historian of our group. Once you get past his frightening appearance, particularly that deep, wide scar that runs like a jagged river straight through the right side of his face with the empty eye socket sitting in its middle, you realize he's probably the most affable of any of us. And the knowledge he shares with the group is invaluable.

Of course, there is some knowledge that is popularly known. In the early days, there were still infrequent transmissions available on television and radio to which we all stayed glued. After those disappeared, there were still the occasional voices of individuals through YouTube or by podcast.

By these means, we learned that the infection had began in the U.S, and it was initially believed that Europe was a safe haven. However, after the first American refugee ships left, reports began to trickle in that Europe was as overrun as North America. I sometimes wonder how those voyages fared. Those boats to Europe were organized by the make-shift militias that popped up after the end became nigh, so they were more filled with arms than people. Maybe they were actually able to survive. Of course, there has been no word.

Dave has been collecting every piece of information he could find since the first sign of the outbreak. It's kind of a driving obsession for him, and I think his house must be filled with creepy scrapbooks on the subject. But I do see the value in that; amidst the chaos, I think it's good that at least someone is trying to keep track of things. There ought to be some record of what has happened to be left for posterity, for humanity's children, if there are any. That's really why I started writing this, I suppose—the desire to leave behind some sort of record of what has happened and of my own existence.

It was from Dave that I learned that there is an underground group of people who have begun to try to salvage mankind's history and piece together what had happened. Within their subculture, an elaborate slang has developed, and a new designation for calendar eras has naturally emerged as part of their lingo: Before Zombie Era (BZE) and Zombie Era (ZE). BZE might as well be prehistoric times at this point. It feels just as far away.

As our meeting began to wind down, without intending to, my gaze kept returning to Tempest. I had to admit a spark of interest in spite of myself. It felt odd. I hadn't had time for anything as frivolous as interest in the opposite sex since ZE began. Why now was this hint of life stirring inside of me? I wasn't even sure where it was stirring. My heart? My loins?

Before I left, I spent a few minutes lingering in a corner staring as nonchalantly as I could manage at Tempest. I just couldn't get enough; I was trying to drink in her image.

I couldn't help myself and was seriously beginning to wonder what the hell was wrong with me. I hadn't been like this, like a teenage boy at the mercy of his raging hormones, in decades.

Chapter 4 - Nothing Left to Lose

Well, I went to the survivor's meeting on a lark and, though I wasn't sure what to expect, it still wasn't what I expected. I guess I thought a group of survivors meeting together would feel empowering in some way, but it really just felt small, enclosed, feeble, and sad.

✦

As I was leaving the meeting, I had a bit of a run-in with the guy named Nathan. Nathan is sort of attractive in an awkward, geek-chic sort of way. He's probably in his early forties, tall and slender, brunette, and a bit scruffy, with floppy hair and two-day stubble from rather adorably haphazard attempts at self-grooming. He has a self-conscious way of carrying himself, as if he's not quite comfortable wearing his own skin. He's the only remotely attractive one of the bunch, of course. Well, actually, Gabe is physically attractive, but even just from briefly speaking to him I can see that the loss of his wife has left him utterly shattered. The loss permeates him, overshadowing his looks and everything else about him. So, realistically, Nathan is the only attractive one. Not that I'm really looking, but still, one can't help noticing these things. I think, if we're honest about it, all people have a fuckability meter against which they measure all new acquaintances of their preferred gender. Nathan may not be at the very top of my scale, but he definitely ranks.

Unfortunately, it turns out that he's a nutcase. He apparently lives with a zombie. I couldn't hold my tongue when I heard someone mention that.

"Wait - you what? You keep a zombie in your house?" I blurted.

"She's my mother..."

"We don't make judgments here." Dave interrupted, trying to neutralize the situation. "This is a safe place where we can speak without shame."

"OK, sure, but at the cost of honesty? None of you are good enough friends to him to explain to him why that's a really bad idea?"

The woman there, Maggie, was looking agitated; her eyes seemed far away and teary.

Dave put a firm hand on my shoulder and just led me away from the group.

So, as usual, I seem to have made a stellar first impression. Anyway, if I'm going to write this, I guess I should do it right. So, I'd best start by officially introducing myself. I am Tempest. Who I was before I became Tempest is of no consequence. She doesn't exist anymore. Tempest is who I am now, and Tempest is strong and free—above all else, free.

After I lost the baby, I stopped caring. It is having nothing to care about, including myself, that has rendered me utterly free in this world. I think it was Janis Joplin that sang "freedom's just another word for nothing left to lose." It's so true.

The thing about stillborns these days is that they don't stay still.

A mother prepares herself to shower her newborn with unconditional love, and then, on a dime, she has to completely alter her thinking and act before her new baby infects her with necrotic scourge.

That babies aren't typically born with teeth is the only saving grace to this situation. Few mothers are actually infected during the course of birth for this reason. Of course, the scent of all that the fresh blood and afterbirth attracts any zombies capable of motility for miles around. A woman still recovering from birth, typically struggling to even stand upright, can find herself in a precarious position, suddenly surrounded by hundreds of the ravenous undead. However, even if she safely escapes the post-labor hordes, the mother of an undead infant is so utterly traumatized by the experience that she frequently takes her own life shortly thereafter anyway.

Apparently whatever umbilical fluid exchange that may occur between mother and child wasn't enough to do me in. Or maybe the baby died only in the last stages of labor. I don't know. I try not to think about it. Or to remember the past. My parents. My sister. My friends and co-workers. My zombie baby gumming my vagina on its way out...

Push it out of my mind. The past no longer exists. Concentrate on the present. Concentrating on the present is the only way to survive.

I've taken on a job of sorts that firmly roots me in the present; it forces me to concentrate on the tasks at hand with no time whatsoever for reminiscing or pontificating. It's difficult to put labels on anything post-apocalypse, but if you had to give my job a name, "bounty runner"

might just about cover it.

I mostly take assignments to procure highly sought after black market goods. It's considered extremely dangerous work, but it pays well in supplies and luxury items. Not that I really care about the pay. I do it because I don't really care about anything. So why not? The thrill of danger produces an adrenaline rush. And when the adrenaline is pumping, at least I know that I'm alive.

When all the seriously bad shit went down a couple of years ago, there were two types of survivors—those who stayed put and those who were uprooted. Most people, at least most of the ones that survived the initial onslaught, were those who were mobile. I suppose remaining stationary was more viable in some places than others. For someone like Nathan, for instance, who lives in the suburbs, staying put would have been a lot easier to pull off because his home must be easier to defend. Though clusters of dead may make it to his residence at times, it has to be nothing compared to the throngs that congregate within the city. Sometimes they are so tightly packed that they form massive walls of dead, an absolute sea of animated bodies.

A lot of people moved at first because these initial migrations were necessary in order to flee the hordes. After that though, most people barricaded themselves in somewhere they deemed fairly safe and have steadfastly remained there since. The average survivor probably doesn't travel more than a few blocks from his or her safe haven. Of course, there are exceptions. For instance, it turns out that, once a month, members of the Survivors typically travel a couple of miles to reach the group's meetings. And since Nathan, that sort-of cute nut job, still lives in his original home in the suburbs, he must have to travel a bit in order to hunt for supplies, but he drives a Hummer and has pre-scouted routes through which he knows he can pass.

But the big exceptions to the shut-in lifestyle are those who are involved with the black market. As one of those, I go pretty much everywhere. While most people sought a safe place to hunker down, some of us adopted the lives of nomads, moving from one location to the next. I guess I like to imagine myself as a ninja, skirting the shadows, scaling buildings (at least figuratively), lithe, agile... I'm sure this little fantasy will probably get me killed one day. Until then, the fantasy makes life a little more fun though, and fun is hard to come by, so I suppose that it's worth it.

The nomadic lifestyle suits me because I have made the conscious decision to let go of everything, both emotionally and physically. I prefer not to let anything get too familiar these days. I move before my surroundings develop too many psychological associations, too many emotional attachments. Objects are infused with our associations—when I looked at a vase in my apartment, I would think of the person who gave it to me, the conversation that I had with my mother about it, the spot where I super-glued it together after my cat clumsily knocked it over... and so on. Every object in my apartment was the same, as were the rooms themselves. Everything familiar was suffused with memories and elicited associated emotions. A clean break from my apartment meant freeing my mind of constant reminders. That place was a memory mill. Give me a sterile white room over that any day. An empty, unfamiliar room is a clean slate; within it, I can purge myself of memories and start fresh once again. By constantly moving and keeping myself busy, there is no time for the past.

～◦⊙◦～

The jobs I take for the black market definitely keep me busy.

There is probably a black market in every major city in the country, but I couldn't say with certainty since I don't know if there are even survivors in other cities. With no communication, this city might as well be the whole world for those of us who survive here.

Our black market functions based upon the work of a network of individuals. The network consists of runners, who obtain desired goods from across the city, delivery guys, who go to people barricaded within their homes to deliver their goods and take new orders, and Jack. Jack is management—he keeps the books, sends out runners for goods, stores the goods, sends out the delivery guys to distribute the goods and collect payments (usually in the form of other desired goods), pays his employees (again, with other goods), and generally gets rich, sitting high on the hog. He has an extensive list of customers— just about every living person in the city. If, in the course of our procuring goods, we run across a survivor, they are added to his list. Everyone wants something, and most have at least something that someone else might want. And Jack gets a cut of every exchange.

Jack also takes some very specific, less savory, requests—sometimes for the occasional dispatch of a troublesome person (living or dead) or for meat (generally it's human, but etiquette dictates that customers don't ask). Mostly though, the lurid requests are for young, attractive female zombies to be used as sex dolls (or young, attractive living females to turn into zombie sex dolls). Why not keep them alive, right? Well, zombies don't have to be fed (What are they going to do, starve to death?). More importantly, most patrons of zombie brothels feel no qualms about shoving their dicks in a non-sentient being. The zombie may be moaning and spluttering behind its gag, but that's more appealing than it pleading and crying. Some men might have second thoughts about raping a living woman, so it's easiest to just kill the women. Lovely, I know. I hate the sex trade, but it's a booming industry, and nothing I can do is going to stop that. Jack doesn't run the sex trade, but he does supply it. A customer is a customer in his book. They order, and he delivers. I'm one of Jack's runners, but I steer clear of any jobs related to that particularly unseemly aspect of Jack's business.

After that odd self-help meeting (if that is what it was), I started my trek back to the my current place of residence, but there was still some daylight, so I decided to postpone returning home. Instead, I took a slight detour, figuring that I might as well kill two birds with one stone. There was a place very nearly on the way that I knew was likely to contain my current quarry: fashion magazines. Go figure. Shut-ins get hankerings for some odd things.

⌒⌒∽⌒⌒

So I diverted course in order to check out an abandoned dentist's office that was about a mile from where I was bunking.

The door was ajar; the office had probably been ransacked shortly after the outbreak had begun. Hospitals, clinics, pharmacies, and anywhere else that contained medications were at the top of the list when the looting began.

Cautiously peering inside, I saw no signs of movement. I pulled my prized flashlight out of my rucksack and turned it on, shining the beam inside.

I hated to even use my flashlight. It was a good quality light torch with a strong beam, and I lived with a constant needling worry in the back of my mind that it eventually, inevitably, would cease to work or that I would simply run out of batteries for it.

The office was, as expected, in a state of disarray. There were patient files strewn across the waiting room's chairs and over the floor. A partial corpse was propped in one very stained corner of the room. Otherwise, the waiting room seemed normal.

I eased in carefully and checked to make sure that there was nothing nasty lurking behind the reception window. Then I began to pick up the files, absent-mindedly wondering if the piece of a body in the corner had once been the receptionist. As I suspected, I unearthed a magazine here and there as I proceeded to gather up loose file papers and folders. I came away with two issues of Cosmopolitan magazine, which would bring me a surprisingly hefty sum, and my efforts also unearthed a few issues each of People, Sports Illustrated, Retirement Magazine, and Parenting Monthly. I took the People and Sports Illustrated, stuffing them into my pack along with the Cosmos. I had no personal interest in them, but they might be sought by customers later. The retirement and parenting magazines were far too cruel a read for our current world climate; they were physical artifacts embodying our collective shattered hopes and dreams. The few children who might still survive were unlikely to ever reach adulthood, and the concept of earning a peaceful retirement was just another heartbreaking relic of a world that was now forever lost. I left those magazines behind, tossing them into the corner with the mangled human remains—both remnants of the bygone era they had once shared, now unceremoniously laid to rest together.

Unfortunately, if things go right for me for too long, I get cocky—and careless.

Coming out of the dentist's office, I wasn't paying attention. I just about walked smack-dab into a staggering, pus-laden bucket of stench that had formerly been a teenage girl. It wasn't exactly fresh—its eyes were gone, and it had long, stringy hair matted to its scalp with oily tufts stuck out in every direction. A good hunk of the zombie's right cheek was gone, exposing a row of its teeth. With a direct view of its dental work, I couldn't help wondering for a brief moment if, in its former life, it had been a patient at this dental office.

The zombie girl pivoted on her heels to face me with relative alacrity. Perhaps the weight of my backpack slowed my reaction time, or maybe I was just more lost in thought than usual, but for whatever reason, I was slow to respond; the zombie's hands were already on my face before I even processed that it was there. Its hands were slimy with rot but with mercilessly jagged, clawing tips. The bones must have been sticking clean out at the ends of its fingers, because fingernails simply aren't that hard. Besides, corpse's fingernails are incredibly dry and brittle (trust me).

I jerked back, thrusting my arms out defensively to push it away from me. My machete was hanging at my side from my makeshift belt, as always. I reached desperately for it with my right hand while trying to keep her at a distance with my left. This wasn't easy; the zombie girl's gaping mouth was hovering dangerously close to my arm as it dove at me again after every shove.

Freeing the machete from my belt, I drew my arm back and then swung down at its head with all my might. The misbegotten zombie girl stopped in mid-lunge, instantly losing animation as the blade connected with brain. She collapsed to the ground, dropping with such force that it wrenched the machete from my hand.

I wiped my hands on my jeans to make sure they were free of zombie goop, then felt my face for scratches. I could feel a couple of scrapes where it had raked its fingertips along my cheeks. Hopefully they were surface abrasions and the skin had not been broken. I cursed under my breath; I wanted to get home now and slather my face with Neosporin.

Bending down, I was able to see the zombie more closely as I removed my machete from its head. Noticing its features, its auburn hair and high cheekbones reminded me a little of my sister. Damn it. There it is—the past, memories of it always slipping in when they aren't wanted.

Not that my sister is dead, necessarily. I put my sister on a boat. Sometimes I let my mind wander to her. I know the odds are against her, against all of us. I don't dare hope. But sometimes I let myself think of her, the one person from my former life that I don't know with certainty has met an end yet. I will never be able to communicate with her again, so I'll never know if she's OK. But I'll never know with certainty that she is dead either. That's the brightest spot I have.

Chapter 5 - Unburdened

I'm not sure why, but I went back for the next meeting. After a month of my standard solitary pursuits, I guess I just wanted the change of pace.

The group's meeting began like the last one: breaking the ice by exchanging meaningless pleasantries, a solemn moment of silence, a brief summary of the minutes of the previous meeting, and then the floor was opened up for members to speak.

Things got heavy quickly this time. Gabe decided to share his story.

Gabe looked to still be in his late twenties and was built; his swollen muscles were positively popping out of his t-shirt. His appearance would have been that of a roughneck if it weren't for the haunted, far-away look in his eyes. It seemed painfully obvious that he was limping around on a broken soul, and I kind of dreaded finding out why.

Gabe began by telling us about his first experience with zombies. He had been an off-shore man. His job required that he spend a month working on the oil rig at a time, then he had a month off before his next shift.

"Imagine," he said, "how we men felt when we came off of that rig."

When they approached the shore, they had found some rather unpleasant looking well-wishers waiting for them to arrive. Sure, the men had wondered why they had lost radio contact a few weeks prior, but they hadn't naturally just jumped to the conclusion that the world had been overrun by zombies just because they were out of contact...

Gabe told us how he and some of his fellow crew survived that initial encounter with the dead, and then he got to his real story. He had been married to a woman named Myra, whom he clearly loved more than anything else in the world.

That's when Gabe really opened up. He told us more about Myra than any of us would ever care to know, including how they met, things they enjoyed doing together before the outbreak, and even tiny little details about her appearance and personality that he found endearing. It was heartbreaking to watch him recount his story. We all nodded at appropriate times and tried to look supportive while we shifted uncomfortably in our chairs and waited for him to reach his conclusion.

But he kept on sharing. We all knew he needed to and indulged him accordingly, but he sure did share *a lot*. God help us, he shared all over the place, and I think that level of brutally raw emotion was almost more than any of us could bear. It was like the flood gate had been opened, and now he couldn't stop talking. The words just came pouring out of him in a stream of consciousness flood. It was all we could do to stand back so as not to be knocked over by the torrent and drown in them.

✧✦✧

Myra was bitten by a zombie, and the bite had gotten hopelessly infected. Gabe's recounting of Myra's last days was particularly upsetting.

"She couldn't speak during the last days. I'm not sure she even understood what was happening at the end. But I'll never forget her big eyes looking up at me as I leveled the gun to her head. It tore my heart apart to pull the trigger, but it was important to me to release her before she became reanimated by the hunger. I still ask myself all the time if I took her too soon. I could have given her a few more hours—maybe even another full day. I'll never shake the feeling that I betrayed her." His voice was choking with emotion.

"Myra declined in front of my eyes, and all I could do was helplessly watch. She depended upon me, but I couldn't protect her, couldn't keep her safe or make her well. And, in the end, I was the one who killed her. I have to live with that, but it was my duty—my responsibility to release her. I'm afraid that she didn't understand that. That will always haunt me. She looked up into my eyes with trust, and I took her last bit of life. But I know that is just my burden... the price to be paid for the love I had."

Maggie clucked sympathetically, beginning to rise from her seat to go to Gabe and comfort him. But he raised his hand, gesturing for Maggie to stay where she was.

"I'm ok." Gabe said, smiling despite the tears in his eyes.

"I was lucky for the time we had together. She was the love of my life. She's gone, and she can never be replaced. I'm still here, so I have to keep going. The rest of my life is simply anti-climactic. It's an epilogue."

"Oh, no!" exclaimed Maggie. "That's simply not the case..." she insisted, stirring agitatedly in her chair.

"It's okay, Maggie. For me, Myra was just the best thing ever. I'm not saying I can't go on without her. What other choice do I have? The world just no longer contains the best thing ever. I'll still live; the world will always just be a little less bright."

"I'm not even saying that I won't ever love again." Gabe assured her. "I might. I'm not opposed to it. It just won't be what I had with Myra. It's rare for two beings to connect so perfectly the way we did. For me, she was the one, pure and simple. I miss the fuck out of her, but I always will. There's no fixing that hole in my heart. Now she's gone, and I just have to go on. That's all. Most days, I still miss her so much I can hardly stand it. But that doesn't make her any less dead. So I just have to keep going."

Gabe had cremated Myra - the ultimate selfless act in this fucked up post-apocalyptic world of ours - to honor the memory of a person so much that you deny yourself and all others the sustenance of the deceased's flesh even though it is viable for consumption.

Listening to Gabe, Ron silently nodded, patting Tex's head. He told me later that he had been trying not to think about how fragile his own relationship was. He knew that he was disproportionately lucky among the group. Unlike Gabe, his primary relationship was intact, nor was it hopelessly twisted, like Nathan's. But dogs don't live forever. What would he do when Tex was gone? The dog was already about eight. Even under ideal circumstances, which these certainly were not, how much more time would Tex have? Four or five more years? Would it still be worth the amount of effort required to survive in this world once Tex was no longer around to share it with him?

I caught Gabe by the arm and privately offered my condolences after he was finished his public emotional purging. Although he was a walking portrait of loss, I guess at least nobody could ever say that Gabe was not in touch with his feelings.

What he said to me caught me off-guard.

"Oh, thanks, but it's okay. Really, it is. I'm just grateful that I didn't take my time with Myra for granted. I knew it was perfect while we were together and cherished every moment we had. I'm glad I didn't squander our time together."

"But you're absolutely tortured. How can you live in constant pain?" I asked him.

"What is the alternative? To make myself forget? Then it would be like I never had the best experiences of my life. Should I choose to paint my entire life grey in order to avoid the black parts?"

Gabe's words gave me a moment's pause. His approach to life was the polar opposite of my own. What had surprised me about his words was that they actually made sense. Of course, it was more clear cut if one had something bright, shining, and beautiful to remember. I didn't think that I did, but I'd shut so much out by now that, at this point, I couldn't even be sure.

After my encounter outside of the dentist's

office, my face had healed, but it had taken longer than I would have liked. One of the scratches the teenage zombie had inflicted upon me had gotten infected. It got red, puffy, and wept for a week before I was able to get it under control. Fortunately, I had a good stash of bandages, ointments, and antibiotics. There are perks to working for the black market.

Unfortunately, although healed, a red mark was still clearly visible across my right cheek, and it started quite a bit of curious chatter in the group.

When I explained that I had suffered a minor laceration at the hand of a zombie (literally), Ron looked at me, aghast.

"You should always tie a rag or bandana around your face to prevent the possibility of infection even from droplets or spatters."

"You're perceiving it wrong." Dave cut in. "It's not a matter of exposure causing infection. We're all already infected. It's a matter of needing to avoid exposure because the bacteria zombies carry is so virulent. A scratch from a zombie can potentially kill you because of the bacteria. Tempest, you were lucky to recover."

"I had supplies." I said, shrugging it off.

"But it doesn't matter what kills a person. Bacteria, starvation, cancer... regardless, everyone is a zombie after death."

Although I wasn't thrilled about my splotchy complexion becoming the focal point of the group's banter, this line of conversation did eventually lead Dave to disseminate some interesting general zombie information.

"We're *all* infected." Dave continued. "That's why we'll come back when we die."

"When the dead bite the living, it's just a virulent bacterial infection that causes the bitten person to die. Then their own infection, or, if you really want to be accurate, mutation, which is already present in their DNA, reanimates them. A zombie's bite is like that of a monitor lizard. The chunk they take out of you might not kill you, but the bacteria from their mouths is likely to do so in short order. The bite kills, but it doesn't cause reanimation."

"But why?" Ron asked. "Why would nobody have this infection and then, suddenly, one day everyone becomes infected? Some alien asteroid? Or a biological weapon? I've heard a million theories since this shit began, but nobody seems to actually know."

"It had something to do with beef." Dave said.

We all looked at Dave, with varying degrees of puzzlement visible on our faces, and waited for him to say more.

"You can only feed cows other cows for so long." Dave said by way of explanation. "All the cutting corners on animal feed and genetic engineering of crops to maximize profits had an unexpected effect. They fed the cows waste, byproducts, genetically modified grain and meal...

You eat enough genetically modified food, it's going to modify your genetics."

"But vegetarians..." Maggie began.

"Vegetarians and those who strictly ate organic foods weren't immune to the infection. Vegetarians typically made the decision to not eat meat in adulthood. They had already consumed heaps of genetically altered plants and animals by then. I mean, hell, it was in the goddamned milk."

Dave had been compiling research since the outbreak began, and now he was able to lay it all out for the layperson, or laypeople in this case—us.

"Scientists kept waiting to see the effects of genetic engineering, but they were looking in the wrong place. They were watching for effects on living human beings, but the mutation it had caused remained dormant during the human life phase. The effect only presented in the post-life phase—the result being that the dead wouldn't stay dead."

"Remember mad cow disease? Beef moguls fed cows the left over bits of other cows, and it altered the animals' protein sequences. People should have seen that something was up then. We fucked up the food supply and poisoned ourselves."

If what Dave said was true, I wondered what

the ramifications would be of our post-apocalyptic diet. Cannibalism had quickly become the norm after the outbreak. The living not only ate each other; they ate zombies if they were still fresh enough to consume. What further genetic damage might we be doing? But maybe that was a moot point; humanity seemed to already be tapering off to its doomed conclusion. Another plague of any sort seemed as though it would just be overkill.

Ron asked, "But why did all the dead start getting up and walking at the same time then? That doesn't make sense... People would have had to be infected for years before the apocalypse occurred."

"Popular theory is that the mutation existed but lay dormant and unnoticed until some precipitating global event triggered activation of the gene. A chemical spill was initially blamed as the cause of dead reanimation, but we now know that it could only have been a catalyst. High levels of some fucked up toxic chemical were carried on the air currents around the world, like radiation from Chernobyl. Though it's difficult to verify anything scientifically anymore, it is strongly speculated that the spill provided the catalytic agent, awakening the gene. If it hadn't been that spill though, something else would have triggered it eventually. It was just waiting for a reason to wake up."

After years of having to accept this horrible reality without knowing why, somehow the availability of a plausible explanation didn't make me feel much better. Still, maybe that there is an ascertainable reason is the first step toward the possibility of there ever being a solution. I'm not optimistic, but maybe.

If his information is accurate, Dave also provided the group with some useful practical knowledge about zombie behavior. He seems to have access to information about research that is being conducted underground, which makes him a very interesting person to know.

Dave told us that zombies primarily hunt by sense of smell.

"A zombie's senses are severely dulled. It doesn't feel pain. Its body only seems to register pressure. And zombies are almost completely blind. Eyes are soft and delicate; they begin to decompose at the moment of death." Dave moved his hand over his eye patch as he spoke, drawing his index finger unconsciously over the grain of the fabric.

"A zombie is lucky if it can discern even vague shapes. Although the eardrums seem to take a long time to cease functioning altogether, hearing also degenerates quickly after death. Although zombies continue to discern loud noises and certain frequency pitches almost indefinitely, their auditory discrimination becomes extremely poor almost immediately."

I couldn't help wondering if there were scientists in a lab somewhere playing sounds to zombies and recording the results. I didn't interrupt to ask Dave though. It seemed like it might come off as rude.

"The olfactory senses seem to be the most resilient post-mortem. Zombies continue to exhibit signs of experiencing smells months, and even years, after death. It is speculated that taste functions similarly."

"Are you saying that if I were cornered by zombies, I could avert being eaten if I were walking around with a slab of rotten meat in my pants?" Ron asked, smirking.

"I don't know. Do you want to test that?" Dave asked

"Nah, I'll pass, thanks."

"One other thing, though—in addition to smell and taste, zombies seem to have one other adequate capability. A zombie's ability to discern heat and cold may be its most enduring sense. Zombies will only eat meat that is raw and warm."

"That *is* true!" Nathan piped up suddenly, and then abruptly went quiet again. Nobody asked him how he knew.

Chapter 6 - Mother's Milk

That girl was at our survivors' meeting again. I know I shouldn't say "girl" but instead "woman," but Tempest is quite a bit younger than I am. She is probably still in her late twenties. Not that age differences matter so much anymore. At least, I don't think they do. Hell, I don't know. I live with my dead mother. What do I know about current dating norms?

But still, it seems as though if two people are both alive, that alone gives them something in common these days. An eighty year old and a twenty year old could conceivably make good companions. Sexual attraction is a secondary consideration. Not that I would want sex to be peripheral for us if Tempest and I were to get together. Far from it. Damn it, I'm digressing.

❦

After I almost put my foot in my mouth during our whole group conversation, members splintered off to chat with one another for a little while longer before we officially adjourned.

Tempest was talking to Dave, but I managed to catch her for a couple of minutes before our meeting ended. And, when she stood up and began to put on her jacket (black leather, of course), the sleeve of her shirt rode up and I was able to get a better look at her tattoo. It is a jet black raven perched on barbed wire. I don't know what that means, if anything, but it's kind of sexy. Not that I would ever want any tattoo myself. And I certainly wouldn't want my daughter to get one. God, I hope my daughter is still alive.

Anyway, the maddening thing about Tempest is that the internal standards that I apply everywhere else are meaningless when it comes to her. She exists outside of the rules. She could have tattoos and piercings, smoke and drink, be an assassin for hire... I'd still accept her and would want to ask her out for coffee.

"I'm glad to see you came back." I said to her.

"Yeah, not sure why, but it stayed on my mind. I'm still not sure if a survivors' support group is even a good idea, but it was too different from my daily routine for me to skip."

She tossed her long blonde hair over her shoulder as she spoke. It was very distracting. I nodded in agreement.

"So, the next meeting is a big shin-dig, huh?" she said, referring to the last order of business we had discussed as a group today.

"Yeah, apparently so. I'm going to bring vegetables from my garden."

"Mmmm, fresh vegetables. Very nice." she said, rewarding me with a smile. I think I melted a little.

Then Dave flung the doors open, and it was time to go. We always left as a group; lingering by oneself was dangerous.

It's possible that I am imagining it, but I feel

as though Tempest and I have definite chemistry. She is damnably cool and aloof, and I feel as awkward as a school kid, but I still think it's there. Maybe it's just because it has been so long, but when I'm around her, I feel more like a virgin than a divorced man in his forties with a long history of sexual experiences.

After today, I have to admit to myself that there is a seed of loneliness that has been growing within me for some time now. I have rather successfully deluded myself that Mother's companionship was enough; certainly, it has at least kept me busy. But I'm no longer able to just refuse to see that a yearning exists within me. Not that there is anything I can do about it right now. There are no singles bars or online dating sites to which I can run. I can only bide my time for a month, and hope that next month's meeting may allow me to come a little closer to knowing Tempest. If she is even there.

I can't say that I was terribly happy to return home.

Mother's "condition" is worsening. Technically, of course, it's the same. Dead is dead, after all. There's no cure for that and no worse she can get. Still, her condition, as in the changes her physical state is undergoing, is definitely worse for me as an observer. I'd say "caregiver," but as much as I may try to be that, I'm completely impotent when it comes to providing care. Anyway, the simplest way I can explain the current problem is that Mother has sprung a leak. Well, more accurately, she has begun to spring multiple leaks, actually, and it's incredibly foul.

From multiple wet, open sores on her body, my mother is leaking noxious, milky, sometimes clumpy, liquid. I don't know what to do about this development, and her leaking wounds smell so horrible that I start to gag whenever I try to even get close enough to examine them.

I'm really trying to be as positive about the situation as I can. If I drape fabric across the window to keep the light dim, and I put big gobs of Vick's under my nose, spending time together can still be almost pleasant. We sit in a near silence that is only broken by the occasional sound of mother shifting on the bed, straining against her bonds, or smacking her moist, open mouth, or the occasional faint sound of trickling liquid.

But there are no words. We don't speak; that's what is important. It's nice without words. When it's silent, there are no buried meanings, no implied accusations. We don't speak of my failings as a son, my failure to protect her. We just sit, in relative peace. Can I give this up? Am I willing to? I think I may have no choice soon. But I fear that the whispered accusations spoken within my own mind may become deafening without having the task of tending Mother to distract me.

As I said, I'm trying to stay positive. Though admittedly mostly it serves as just a much-needed means of distraction, I have been throwing myself into gardening with renewed enthusiasm lately.

Ever since the outbreak, I have tried to grow whatever I can with the little packets of stale seeds that Mother had on hand, plus any others I have since been able to scavenge. The problem is that the plants that grow won't reproduce. The plants have been genetically altered so that, even though they reach maturity, they are not able to produce fertile seeds. In the last decade prior to the End Time, the one and only big multi-national seed company, which had had a monopoly on world-wide seed distribution, had ensured its hold on the market by rendering all of its plants incapable of reproduction. Somehow, that was legal. So all of the plants that I am able to grow are sterile. It makes for real problems now.

I keep a little garden in the backyard. Gardening is a very calming activity; there is something peaceful and comforting about working with the soil. It's important for me not to get so lost in it that I let my guard down while I'm doing it though.

My garden plot actually produces relatively little—certainly not enough for me to sustain myself with it— but every little bit helps. It's nice to have fresh vegetables, an occasional squash here, some spinach there...

My repertoire includes squash, carrots, spinach, broccoli, green beans, and sunflowers. The sunflowers are entirely impractical—their seed yield doesn't justify the space they occupy, but I love the way they look. They remind me of my childhood.

There was no real way for me to keep the dead out of my garden, though they wander in only infrequently. It doesn't really matter though—it's not like they are going to eat anything there. In fact, if anything, they probably help to fertilize the plot.

∽≈⊙≋∾

About a week has passed since the last Survivors meeting, which I suppose is what I measure time against these days.

In the past week, Mother has gotten much worse. Especially today.

I have been up since early this morning when Mother began making disturbing (more disturbing than usual) noises. She has been spluttering non-stop for hours now, making aspirated gurgling sounds that are expelled from in her throat in forceful wet chaotic bursts.

In the past, I had considered trying to find a ball gag for Mother in one of the several abandoned sex emporiums off of the highway. However, her mouth has just kept widening as she has continued to decay, so it would have had a very limited period of usefulness. I have often thought in passing about how quickly it would have just been swallowed up, disappearing into her damp, black viscous maw. I am reminded of this again now because she sounds as though she could be choking on a ball gag now. If one could choke endlessly, for hours upon hours, on a ball gag...

I'm so very tired. Physically, but even more so emotionally. There are only so many hours of the worst things imaginable that one can witness before beginning to grow numb. Mother has been spluttering and thrashing, splattering dark, sticky droplets of liquid that makes me retch across everything in the room, including me. In the dim light within her room, I can make out the wiggling maggots that have been strewn across the sheets in her convulsions.

CRXODCR

I'll just keep wiping her down. What else can I do? The things that are growing between the moist folds of her flesh... well, there's nothing I can begin to say. These intimate places should never be seen by a son, even when they are fresh, healthy, and living. I shudder involuntarily, try to think of other things, tell myself that I'm somewhere else, but, ultimately, it's my duty as a son and has to be done all the same.

I just keep mopping up the fetid liquid that continuously seeps from Mother with every rag, towel, and sponge that I can find. I don't know where she is holding it all. Her desiccated little corpse should logically be capable of holding only a finite amount of liquid volume. Yet Mother's sour, rancid milk seems to pour endlessly from her. And so I endlessly dab.

CRXODCR

I consider myself a dedicated son, but even I am beginning to see that this is not a sustainable existence. The conditions of our home life have been less than ideal for a long time, but they have taken a sharp downturn. I have to admit that this is deplorable.

Can I continue to live like this? Can I even justify trying to keep Mother under these circumstances? I know it must be wrong to continue this. What for? For the sake of memories? To sustain a routine? To preserve the illusion of a relationship that is already dead?

I am so very tired. I need to sleep. Maybe then I will be able to think more clearly.

Chapter 7 - The Winds of Change

Lately, Jack has been making some choices that I consider very questionable. Most notably, he has brought into his operation some jackass thug kids that I suspect are also wrapped up in the sex trade. I'm not sure why he needs middlemen now when he never did before, but it is what it is, I guess.

When I showed up at Jack's warehouse yesterday, a kid at the front door directed me to see "Bobby" for my assignment. Bobby is apparently handling assigning jobs to runners now; I guess Jack needs more time to count his spoils.

Bobby was maybe nineteen years old, dressed in army fatigues (which ironically did not blend in well at all in our urban environment) and sneakers, and had a fresh buzz cut. When

I entered his office, he was drinking from a bowl made out of the top of a human skull. I introduced myself curtly, unconsciously making a face as I watched him drink.

Seeing that I had recoiled, he proudly said "I use everything from what I kill, like the Native Americans." punctuating his remark with a smugly pleased smirk.

"So did Hitler." I said, not batting an eye. "There's a difference between being efficient and being just plain gruesome. It's not like there's a shortage of pottery available to loot."

He ignored me, returning to the job at hand.

My new mission was straight-forward enough. A former client had been reported by one of our delivery people as recently deceased. Bobby didn't say how the client had died, but she was apparently elderly, so my guess was associated health complications. My job was two-fold. I needed to dispatch her reanimated corpse and to reclaim all goods of value from her apartment. The woman had been a big consumer of black market medical goods and had apparently had a healthy supply of dry goods such as powdered milk with which to trade. There should be quite a bit worth taking in her apartment. This was standard practice when a client perished.

I left with the unfortunate woman's address. It was still early in the day, and the sky was clear, so I figured that there was no time like the present.

Things wound up being a lot less clear cut after I got to the former client's residence.

Standard delivery procedure was to knock on an accessible door or window and identify oneself in a loud voice. This procedure was useless under current conditions, of course. The old woman inside was no longer capable of opening a door, and alerting her (it) to my presence wasn't really advisable. My best course of action was to find the entrance that offered the least resistance and brandish my crowbar at it.

The windows were solidly boarded up, so I settled for the back door; it was equipped with only a flimsy lock. I've been doing this sort of thing for some time now, so it didn't take very long for me to gain entry. Unfortunately, in doing so, I wasn't exactly quiet.

Something was waiting to greet me when I entered. Its white hair, with curlers dangling askew from it, framed its face like an absurd, ghostly halo. The old woman was probably a few weeks dead; the forces of decomposition had just begun to take a firm hold in her carcass. Lumps of larvae visibly wriggled beneath the skin of her limbs as she stretched them out toward me.

The zombie was ambling slowly; judging from the metal walker in the corner of the room, its bodily movement had been limited prior to death. I planted my feet wide, bracing myself to swing the crowbar against its skull as it stepped closer.

There was a deafening clap like thunder, and the zombie pitched forward, spraying coagulated goop, brain, skin, hair, and skull fragments all over the front of my shirt.

Involuntarily letting out a shriek, I jumped backwards, completely startled and confused, and knocked over the walker as I pressed myself into the corner of the room.

From the doorway came a man's voice. "What the fuck? Who is there?"

A rifle appeared in the doorway. Behind it, a young man of about eighteen in a tattered t-shirt and jeans followed.

Seeing me, he said "Who the fuck are you?"

I was still catching my breath, but I managed to choke out my name.

"What are you doing here?" he asked, eyeing me suspiciously. Then he added, "Your shirt is completely disgusting."

"Yeah," I gasped, "it was a lot cleaner when I got here. I'm a runner. I was sent to kill *that*." I said, gesturing to the headless remains of the old woman that was occupying a prominant portion of the room's carpet.

"Bullshit." he said, but he lowered the barrel of his rifle toward the floor.

"Killing *that*," he said, gesturing to the crumpled carcass, "is *my* job."

"You're a runner?" I asked, perplexed.

"Yeah." the young man said. "Have been for a couple months. Name's Drew." He slung the rifle over his shoulder and then ran his hand through his greasy, mussed dirty blonde hair.

"Who do you work for?" I asked.

"Jack. Who else?" he replied. "But Bobby assigned me the job. You?"

"Yeah, same." I said, feeling myself deflate.

Fuck. Two runners assigned to the same job? You've got to be kidding me. I almost got killed by this kid. This was bullshit.

Was Bobby planning to pay us both? Now that was an unlikely scenario. Was he expecting us to fight it out? Or to accidentally kill each other? The most likely explanation was probably just poor management. Bobby didn't exactly inspire confidence, so that it was just a stupid fuck-up on his part was certainly possible.

The boy had already obtained a good deal of the supplies and had dispatched the former client, so I guess the score was his. I didn't feel like arguing about who had more claim, and not just because he was better armed than I was. I had my crowbar, the machete at my hip, and a handgun in my jacket, but a gunfight wasn't something in which I was interested in engaging. And there was no reason. It wasn't the kid's fault. And it wasn't worth fighting over the payload any single mission could yield. The bigger picture was troubling though. This turn of events put my whole employment situation in question in my mind.

I don't particularly need my job with the black market. Over the past couple of years, it has afforded me a plethora of premium supplies, but I could get by, though more meagerly, without it. To be honest, I've been putting myself in danger as much for the sake of the adrenaline rush as for the material rewards. It was an effective, and at times exhilarating, way to prove to myself that I'm still alive. And I have been developing mounting concerns as Jack had gotten more intertwined with the sex trade, but it still seemed distant enough for me to keep it in the back of my mind. Now I must begin to consciously ask myself: is this really sustainable? Can I go on indefinitely like this? Eventually, odds are that I'll slip up and get critically injured or killed outright. And that's just the danger inherent in relying upon myself. A screw up seems fairly inevitable. But Jack putting jackass kids in charge elevates my danger level quite a bit, whether due to their incompetence, lack of experience, or just general lack of concern for my fucking well-being.

Well, food for thought. I shook Drew's hand, wished him well, and headed home. I was anxious to change my clothes.

Stealthily making my way home through back alleys, I started thinking about Nathan again. Damn it. His face spontaneously popped into my head. Something about him is definitely sort of cute. Why is he getting under my normally tough skin? Maybe things are just in a state of flux. In joining the silly survivor group, I have adopted a new routine. And things are getting weird with the black market. Things are changing, so maybe I am too. I need to be careful; I can't afford to get careless.

At the very least, I need to take a little break before I take on any new black market assignments. Fortunately, I already placed an order for the meat for our next Survivors meeting. I arranged it earlier this month in lieu of payment for a job.

The meat will be human, of course. Zombie human, more than likely. The memory of what animal meat even tasted like has already faded.

❧

Animals don't reanimate. Thank god for small favors, right? They don't seem to possess the mutation or whatever it is that causes humans to pop back up after death. Bottom line, animals just lay there peacefully and stay dead. Unfortunately though, the living now have to compete with the dead for animals as a food source. The dead aren't terribly discriminating about their eating habits. If it has life, it will make an appealing meal.

Since the living are in competition with the dead for animals as food, and because people are no longer producing meat by the tons and pumping it into the cities via eighteen wheelers twenty-four hours a day, there aren't a lot of animals to be found anymore. Most of them seemed to get devoured in the first few months -

either by the living or the dead. Birds twittering on phone lines, squirrels scampering up trees, and rats scurrying around in alleys are no more than distant memories now. I guess maybe it's different in rural areas. Having spent my whole life in cities or suburbs, I really couldn't say. Perhaps, if farmers are diligent enough in defending their livestock from the meandering undead hordes, they might actually be able to eke out a sustainable existence by breeding and raising livestock. I can't really imagine that being possible in the United States even before the zombie era, but as I said, I'm no expert.

It's not of particular relevance to me anyway. In the city, my world, there is virtually no access whatsoever to any animals anymore. The pre-apocalypse staples of the American diet, beef and poultry, stopped being available as soon as the outbreak occurred. There are no waterways within at least fifty miles of me that haven't been contaminated by industrial waste for decades, so fishing is not a viable possibility. And I won't eat pet flesh. An animal is far more innocent and genuine than any human being. Besides, eating a dog is an unthinkable taboo in our post-apocalyptic culture. Dogs are far too valuable. Sure, the larger breeds are revered as protectors, but even the smallest toy or teacup serves as an invaluable zombie alarm. A lot of survivors eat cats, if they can catch them. I won't. I like them far too much. But I suppose it's much easier to be principled when you're only talking about a yield of maybe a pound or two of meat once the feline is skinned and deboned. Turning one's nose up at a human meal is a great deal more difficult to do.

It's funny how fast our biggest taboos can become passé when circumstances change. I'm sure that in our former lives, every one of us would have passed judgment on the practice of cannibalism, summarily condemning all that would resort to it under any circumstances. "Surely there is a less barbaric solution." we would tut.

We live in a different reality now, and we can never return to our previous one. There are no solutions that are not barbaric. The average human diet is perhaps eight hundred calories a day. We're all gaunt, and we take our sustenance wherever it may be found.

I would imagine that eating another human being is like committing murder, bestiality, incest, or any of our other societal taboos—the first time is the monumental hurdle. Once you've done it once, the boundary has been crossed. You've already irreparably altered who you are. There is no going back. After that, you can quickly come to view it as normal, unremarkable behavior.

Chapter 8 - Another One Bites...

We're celebrating. It is technically the group's two year anniversary, although there were apparently only two members for the first few months, and both of them are now dead.

Still, we'll take the opportunity to give thanks wherever we can find it.

The Survivors of the Apocalypse hold every meeting in a different location. It was decided that it just seems safer to do it that way, although I'm not sure why.

Today, we met in an abandoned high school. Schools were closed when signs of the outbreak first appeared, so except for the few that were turned into evacuation centers, they are generally surprisingly safe, deserted, and zombie-free. In fact, schools would probably make excellent safe havens for clans of survivors to colonize if their fences were just more sturdy.

We began by setting up in the cafeteria. Maggie dressed a long folding table with a tasteful, relatively unstained white table cloth and decked it out with what remained of her wedding china.

As timid and meek as Maggie is, it's difficult to imagine her making the trek to this school loaded down with serving dishes and cutlery. I guess it's all a matter of where your priorities lie. I involuntarily shook my head from side to side in mild dismay as if I were trying to dislodge from my mind the absurd image of Maggie darting between buildings in her house dress and support stockings with a pack full of dishes strapped to her back.

I brought the meat. Considering the nature of the jobs I typically took to keep busy, skimming a little extra was generally pretty easy. But this I had actually paid for, and it showed.

It was a good cut—from a specimen that was neither emaciated nor too fatty. People who had fattened themselves on fast food before the zombie era began typically tasted absolutely terrible—tasteless, greasy, tough, full of gristle, and frequently riddled with tumors. It was rare that you got a hold of healthy, lean human meat. I don't know, maybe that was because those were typically the people who were still alive.

Jack said that this meat came from a young man in his twenties who was found hobbling around on a severely injured leg. A bounty runner had taken him out before zombies took him down or the infection in his leg spread and spoiled the rest of him. The story was probably a lie; it was standard practice to dole lies out liberally with meat purchases to help alleviate diner's guilt. Still, I appreciated the story. I try to maintain moral standards, or at least tell myself that I do. It's just important to set personal boundaries, however arbitrary they might seem, in order to maintain a sense of sanity, order, decency... those with no personal code become monsters very easily. So, when it comes to the living, my rule is no women, no kids, and nobody who doesn't obviously have blood on their hands. I've never had much trouble justifying ridding the world of one less bastard. With any person that is already dead, or soon to be dead, all bets were off, of course - anyone is fair game under those circumstances.

I had grilled up a little of the meat ahead of time and tasted it. It was so tender that I wouldn't have been surprised if person it came from had been a vegetarian before the zombie era began. Now, of course, nobody had the luxury of being a vegetarian. You took protein whenever, and wherever, you could find it.

Nathan brought vegetables, as he had promised—a beautiful carrot and spinach salad and fresh steamed broccoli. In my previous life, I'd never really liked the smell of broccoli, but now even the tiniest whiff of it was making my mouth water like crazy.

Ron brought an unopened package of Oreos, some powdered mashed potatoes, and the Sanka. Oreos! Like divine sandwich cookie manna from heaven—I couldn't believe he had managed to find a whole package of them.

Gabe brought cans of beets, beans, and fruit

cocktail. And, I have no idea how Dave did it, but he made a damned pie for the occasion. Cherry.

Maggie, of course, brought her entire kitchen cabinet plus, bizarrely enough, elegant linen napkins. It's the end of the world, and Maggie still uses cloth napkins. It blows my mind. While setting up, she also found for us a couple of enormous cans of applesauce that were left in the cafeteria storeroom. One of them wasn't even puffy.

Dave ushered in what he dubbed our "Survivors' Thanksgiving," and we all seated ourselves around the table.

I have to say, even though I didn't know them too well, the dinner was a moving experience—a rare tender moment between a group of human beings. In this callous, unfeeling world, I had forgotten that moments like these could even happen anymore.

Smiling, laughing faces glowed around that cafeteria table as we all enjoyed the biggest feast in which any of us had partaken in years. It was terribly corny, but we went around the table saying for what each of us was thankful. I think we all were in agreement that we were thankful for the amazing meal, for each other's company, and for being alive.

After we ate, we all embraced. Nathan approached and wrapped his arms around me, brushing his scruffy cheek against mine.

Sensing my receptiveness, he said "I thought that you thought I was a psycho freak." , still squeezing me.

"We all have our foibles. I figure it doesn't pay to be too picky during an apocalypse." I replied, squeezing back.

We all hugged each other after the meal. When Tempest approached me, she leaned in and kissed me on the cheek.

I said, "I thought you thought I was nuts."

"Nah," she said. "We all have our quirks. I figure it doesn't pay to be too picky during the apocalypse." Then she squeezed me tightly.

After dinner and a period of lethargic digestion, we held a short group session. Tempest actually told her story, or part of it anyway. I won't repeat what she said. It was heart-wrenching, and I feel like now I kind of understand why she is so tough.

But Maggie grew uncharacteristically hard and unsympathetic. Tempest's story obviously had hit a nerve for her.

"It could have been worse." she said, her lips pursed as though she had just tasted something bitter.

"Oh?" Tempest said incredulously.

Maggie was glaring at her, staring her down.

Trying to keep her calm, Tempest said "I know that *everyone* has shocking horror stories in this world in which we are forced to live, but I still can't help bristling at having my own treated so dismissively. It's rude to brush aside anyone's pain as a lesser trauma, and I wouldn't do that to you, Maggie."

"It could have been much worse." Maggie said with unusual conviction. "My daughter had a baby shortly before the outbreak—one that lived."

Tempest said nothing, regarding Maggie stonily but waiting for her to continue.

"He was sick—just a cold, we thought—a little cough and a runny nose. But after the outbreak, my daughter and I were constantly on the run with her children. It was an added stress to his system."

"Our food supply was poor; my daughter, like most people at that time, wasn't getting a lot of nutrients. Trevor, her baby, just wasn't getting better. He had gotten pale and was sleeping more than usual, but neither of us realized how sick he really was."

"My daughter was nursing him. The infant had become..." Maggie paused and then corrected herself. *"My grandson,"* she said, emphasizing the words, "had become listless."

It was clear to everyone that Maggie was still engaged in a long-running internal battle to keep distance between herself and the events she was describing.

"Trevor had become uninterested in nursing, so my daughter was initially excited when he actually latched on with gusto to feed."

Maggie looked at the floor, the wrinkles in her face overlapping each other as her expression briefly contorted.

"Of course, the joy turned to horror quickly." she continued, recomposing herself, consciously reassembling her facial expression.

"Trevor had died in my daughter June's arms while still making faint attempts at suckling; he faded away just as though he were falling asleep. Then he returned—reanimated—and chewed off half of her breast before she was able to get him loose.

"How?" Tempest asked, her brows knit. "How did he bite?"

"He was teething." Maggie responded sharply.

"Once June threw him on the floor, the baby was no longer really a threat. Just being dropped probably broke quite a few of his little bones. All he could do was try to crawl pathetically toward our ankles. I just used a broom to push him into another room and then latched the door."

"My daughter was on her knees, writhing in agony. I dressed the wound and tended her as best I could. June, of course, was hysterical, completely inconsolable. But I wasn't there the

109

moment she died. I was... Well, June died and returned, and she was eating Abigail's face by the time I came out of the restroom." Maggie concluded, looking away.

Abigail was Maggie's granddaughter—the granddaughter that Maggie still kept.

Having previously noticed that Maggie goes to the bathroom frequently during even our brief meetings, I have suspected for some time that she has bladder control issues. I could not have guessed that she might blame herself for the death of her granddaughter let alone that herfrequent need to pee might have been responsible for the loss of the child.

"I had to take June out to save myself." Maggie said, her voice monotone. "After that, I stomped the baby to death in a fit of fury."

Her eyes were trained on the floor.

"But I preserved Abigail." she said in a small voice.

So now Maggie was preserving her granddaughter as the last shred of her legacy.

Maggie abruptly got up from where she was seated, turned on her heels, and hurried out of the cafeteria.

"Is she coming back?" Dave asked.

"She left all her china." Tempest observed.

We waited five minutes or so, but she didn't come back.

"I guess we should go after her?" Tempest suggested, although she didn't sound overly concerned.

We gathered up our things as quickly as we could and, as a group, went to find Maggie. She had a head start, so there was a chance we wouldn't catch up to her. I wish that had been the case.

I guess the high school must have had a groundskeeper that lived on the premises. Or maybe it was just a wandering zombie that had gotten in through a hole in the fence. I don't know. I only know that it had torn Maggie apart. Her upper body was at the northern end of the sidewalk outside of the gym, her lower body

111

was at the southern end, and her entrails were strewn all the way between the two.

The zombie was hunched over Maggie's torso gorging itself. Tex knocked it to the ground in short order. Then Ron decapitated it, and that was that.

Maggie's death was so stupid, senseless, and avoidable. And, just like that, our group begins to dwindle once again. Deflated, we all quietly took a portion of Maggie for later consumption, told each other goodbye, and parted.

Chapter 9 - Letting Mother Go

Of course, being an old woman, my mother had already lost a good deal of her muscle tone before she died. Whatever discernible musculature she had left disappeared almost immediately after she expired. Unfortunately, the degradation of her body by no means ended with the loss of muscle tone. The flesh soon became unnaturally soft, like excessively puffy marshmallow, and later still, the meat began to visibly separate, dangling loosely from her.

I suppose what has happened now is the next logical step in the process. I just hadn't let myself consider the natural progression of her body's physical decline. As far as I'd previously observed, zombies typically remain in the bloat or early stages of active decay almost indefinitely. But something seems to have changed. I don't know if Mother is an isolated case, or if all zombies have a similar shelf life, so to speak, but she is deep into what I can only describe as accelerated decomposition now and is rapidly approaching a state of advanced decay; soon very little of her is going to be left.

Like over-cooked chicken, her meat has begun to fall away from the bone. The muscles of her right leg came completely loose from the bone today—hamstrings, quadriceps, calf muscles—all of it just slid off, at most hanging fast here and there by bits of tendon.

I've tried to clean up as best I can. The meat is slimy, and the smell is unbearable. I've had to vomit so many times that I've lost count. And the whole time, as I try to clean around her, Mother writhes on the bed and tries to claw at me. It's a miracle that she hasn't broken my skin. Still, it will be a bigger miracle if just handling such volatile, bacteria-laden refuse doesn't kill me anyway.

As horrible as this has all been, I have the ominous sinking feeling that it could get much worse at any moment. I'm worried that, if the flesh continues to fall off of Mother like this, she may shed enough of her hands and feet to slip out of her bonds.

But that's something I will save to worry about tomorrow. My stomach muscles are sore from retching, and it's time for me to sleep.

I slept on it, and came to an unpleasant but inevitable conclusion. Living with Mother as I have been is no longer a workable arrangement. I was willing to accept an element of danger as long as our lifestyle together was sustainable, but it no longer is. It is rapidly hurtling toward a disastrous conclusion.

I smashed in her head. It didn't put up a lot of resistance— I think it was organically more than ready to be mush.

I buried her in the garden. She's fertilizer now. "From death comes life." The earthworms shall inherit the earth, I guess.

I thought I would be overwrought afterwards,

but I actually experienced an eerie sense of calm. I hate to admit it, but I felt relieved that it was over.

I guess what I honestly miss most is just sitting in the room and knowing that she was there next to me. As I read, I always took comfort in being reminded of her presence by the little sounds of her throat rattling and the gentle rustling of the fabric of her faded housedress as she struggled against her bonds.

I had boarded up all of the windows in the house when the End Time began, of course, but after Mother died, I removed the boards from the window in her bedroom. I figured that she could use the sunlight, I guess, and it wasn't like a zombie wandering through would find her enticing if it noticed her. I kept Mother's bedroom door locked, so I figured that the danger to me was minimal.

Alright, in retrospect, maybe that wasn't a great idea. I've never had a swarm descend upon my property, but I know that doesn't mean it could never happen. If hundreds of the dead piled into my mother's room, I doubt that the lock on the door would hold them out of the rest of the house for very long. Still, I get so few stragglers near my yard these days, and I really did like having natural light by which to read... Candlelight strains my eyes, and candles are a limited commodity.

Anyway, I boarded up the window again. I couldn't bear to sit in there now. The room is far too empty. Besides, it smells really bad.

Chapter 10 - So It Goes

Jack was murdered. Another runner I know stopped by my apartment to let me know. I guess it was inevitable. If you're at the top of the heap, someone beneath you is bound to make a stab at gaining what you have. In this case, a group of young thugs involved in the sex trade slit Jack's throat. Then they apparently roasted him and threw a little party for their buddies. Now they've taken over his warehouse, his stockpile of goods, and his client list. Runners and delivery guys still retain their jobs, but I'm done. My contractual jobs for the black market have finally come to an end.

It's just no longer a workable arrangement. I was willing to accept an element of danger along with my missions—hell, I even embraced it—as long as I had a reasonable chance at succeeding, but that is no longer the case. Even if I kept my eyes glued to the floor, said "yes sir" to that bunch of snot-nosed kids, and took every god-awful job they gave me, my days would still be numbered. My employment is rapidly hurtling toward a disastrous conclusion, and when I'm "terminated," I won't just get fired. Besides, It's not that I was so attached to Jack, but I just can't work for these assholes. Compared to them, Jack was highly principled. I can't in good conscience directly work for these sex trade fuckers.

Rather than slink away, I decided to face them. Fucking kids. Kids with way too much power.

It didn't go over so well.

"Well, that's just fine, Sister. You can be a lot more useful to us in other ways anyway." Bobby said as he advanced toward me, unsheathing a long hunting knife. Thank god he was a slimy bastard who liked to get personal when he killed. I'd be dead if he had just pulled a gun.

I turned and ran, bolting through his office door

and startling several of his lackeys. Fortunately, none of them processed the situation very quickly. It didn't occur to them to chase after me until Bobby ran out of the office and yelled at them to catch me.

I worked for Jack a long time, and apparently I knew the warehouse's layout better than its new owners did. I was able to put some additional distance between myself and my pursuers by zigzagging through areas of the warehouse. I shot through a side door, ran down a corridor, ducked into a store room, and was out through a back stairwell before they could catch up.

The fact is, though, that I barely made it out of there. And I can never go back now, especially since I kind of wrecked one of their store rooms by kicking over a few full floor-to-ceiling shelves to slow them down.

Hopefully, Bobby won't bother to put a bounty out for me.

I returned home and consoled myself with a meal of meat left over from our last Survivors meeting. It was still good because I salted it. We salt the meat to make it last. After all, who has refrigeration these days? Eating meat that has started to spoil is a mistake most survivors have made, I would wager. Meat is too tempting, and it's never easy to gauge how long is too long for it to sit out. But nothing sucks quite like having to run from zombies when you have explosive diarrhea.

Even with a hearty dose of protein, I couldn't shake the troubled feeling I had. It's not like I really cared about that job. It was something to do. And it's certainly not like I really cared about my employers. They were Machiavellian scumbags whose loyalty and kindness was predicated upon my usefulness. Even Jack had probably just been waiting to double-cross me the first time it was advantageous for him to do so.

I don't really think I'm worth paying a bounty to Bobby. Besides, I can move in a heartbeat. I'm not so easy to locate. So why do I feel deflated, vaguely sad, and empty? I guess it's just a result of seeing one more thing come to its inevitable end.

Chapter 11 - Meeting Adjourned

The survivors all looked decidedly less cheerful as we began this month's meeting. We were all still reeling a bit from the sudden gory conclusion to our last gathering.

∾≈⧫≈∾

Nathan arrived a few minutes after I did.

"Hey." I said, waving.

He came over to where I was standing, hugged me, and asked "How are you doing?"

"Oh, you know, I'm still trudging along. I'm only dead on the inside." I said, proffering my best ironic smile.

Nathan frowned. As he did so, I could see the faint wrinkles that were beginning to form around his eyes and mouth. It was oddly endearing, but he looked so saddened by my response that I felt compelled to say more.

"That's not as bad as it sounds." I assured him. "As long as you keep your body alive, I figure that the spirit can always return later. It's a contingency plan. If the world around me ever becomes bearable later, I'll be all ready to go. In the meantime, I just have to keep my momentum—to keep pushing myself forward."

I guess that was exactly what I had been doing for a long time now—just propelling myself forward.

Looking lost in thought, Nathan replied, "Momentum can't be a long term solution, Tempest. You have to find something to care about or you'll die—if not physically, at least on the inside."

"Having nothing to protect means having absolute freedom." I offered.

"Having nothing worth protecting is having nothing worth living for." he countered.

We were both silent for a moment. We seemed to have managed to sum up our two disparate approaches to life pretty accurately. And we hadn't even officially begun the meeting yet. God help us if this was a harbinger of things to come. The weight of this meeting might just form a black hole that sucks up everything around it, pulling us all in. Oh, well. Good riddance if it did.

I patted Nathan on the arm, intending to reassure him and diffuse some of the heavy vibe.

He smiled at me, but it was a sad smile.

We were flirting, which was nice, but the conversation had gotten more intense than I would have hoped. And it wasn't going to lighten up anytime soon.

"I'm sorry about asking this, but it has been on my mind. Would you stuff her?"

"What?"

"Your Mother. If she weren't animated. Would you stuff her? I mean like taxidermy—stuff her corpse and keep her around—like a doll or a collectible? A keepsake?"

I recoiled. "God, no. That's very Norman Bates. I wouldn't do that."

A smile gently tugged at one corner of Tempest's mouth.

"It's the same thing, isn't it? You're keeping her physical body, Nathan, but she's long dead. She's just a creepy sentimental memento. Unfortunately, it's really kind of worse than having a brittle corpse propped up in bed though because she's a dangerous, animated memento."

"As I said before, I think that you have to find something to care about or you die—at least on the inside. For a long time, I wanted to make that something my mother. Having said that though, I think you should know that I put Mother down. Her remains are at rest now."

I was surprised by how calm I was while talking about this formerly touchy subject. A month ago, the conversation would have had me squirming.

"Oh, I'm sorry?" Tempest said, her voice rising to transform the words into a question at the end.

"Nothing to be sorry about. It needed to be done a long time ago."

"Well, I'm glad then. Relieved. It's for the best for you."

"I know. Thanks."

I knew she was right. I had known even when it was the last thing that I had wanted to hear, and I respected her for having been the only one brave enough to say it to me.

Dave called the meeting to order. As we turned to join the circle, Tempest clasped my hand in hers and squeezed.

The meeting this month was inside a university library. The university had been closed when the first signs of outbreak occurred and had remained largely free of looting. Maggie had suggested it before the conclusion of our last meeting, and we had all agreed, figuring that it would offer a exceptional opportunity for book scavenging.

After a moment of silence for Maggie, the minutes were read, and then the floor was opened. Ron began to tell a story about Tex's latest exploits, patting the dog's head affectionately as he spoke.

Almost immediately, Ron was drowned out by a series of cacophonous noises. It sounded like a succession of things crashing, shattering, and clattering.

"What the hell?" Gabe said.

Dave rose and went to the nearest window to see what was happening.

In addition to the sound of things breaking, there seemed to be a low hum. Or maybe it was more like the soft moaning of an ominous wind.

"It should be safe—nobody has been here since the dead first rose." Ron said.

"Was it empty at that time?" I asked with an intentional edge in my voice.

Still looking out of the window, Dave said "It looks like we're pretty damned far from safe at the moment."

We all rushed to the window to see for ourselves.

There was a full-fledged herd of zombies in the yard below us, and they had apparently caught whiff of the living—us—nearby. They were moving slowly because of the poor conditions of their bodies, but they were definitely moving, in mass, toward our location. Some of them were even visibly raising their heads as if they were looking up at us.

University classes, of course, had been cancelled at the first sign of trouble. Shortly after, the university's gates had been closed. But it seemed that, in the confusion and panic that had ensued when the outbreak first began, nobody considered that people might be on campus even if school wasn't in session. These people, probably mostly dorm residents, must have been trapped inside the grounds and simply forgotten. And here they were—falling apart—literally. Three year dead zombies are a pretty pathetic lot. But, although they were excessively decomposed, with hundreds of them, we still didn't stand a chance.

"Shit." Ron said.

Tex was beginning to growl.

Offering his assessment of our situation, Dave matter-of-factly commented " We're going to be overwhelmed and subsequently consumed."

Gabe looked on silently.

Nathan exhaled slowly. "How much time do you think we have before they reach us?"

Nobody even bothered to suggest that we barricade the doors. The first floor was comprised mainly of glass windows. What the hell had we been thinking, really? Greed was the only explanation I could come up with for our blatant eschewing of common sense safety standards.

Greed and gross complacency. We had all gotten careless. Seeing Maggie in pieces should have at least put us on our toes, but we had been imprudent and lackadaisical nonetheless.

Our last few minutes before the zombie horde reached us were spent fruitlessly looking for makeshift weapons to augment our normal gear (I had my standard machete and handgun) or hunting for a cubbyhole in which to hide.

Then the dead were at the doors. They had hardly any strength left in their limbs, so individual zombies striking the glass produced little effect. But the sheer weight of them as more and more pressed forward quickly began to crack the glass. It gave under the crush of their weight, and then they were inside.

Nathan reached out and grabbed me, protectively wrapping his arms around me, placing his own body between me and the herd. As a meat shield, Nathan wouldn't slow that army of the undead down for more than maybe a minute or two at most. But even in the midst of this crisis, I was overwhelmed by that silly fool's valiance. He was a goddamned comic book hero. I loved him at that moment.

The throng was advancing. The most agile, intact zombies were at the front; impaired, partial zombies proceeded with greater difficulty, often crawling. They made up the rear of the horde's haphazard formation.

Dave was the first to go down. I saw his arms briefly flailing, and then his body sank out of sight as the sea of the dead surrounded him and swallowed him up.

Nathan had a tight grip on my hand.

"Follow me!" he urged, pulling me toward the reading rooms. As we ran toward them, I heard the sound of Tex yelping inconsolably.

Things went from bad to worse very quickly. I pulled Tempest along with me as I headed for the reading rooms. There was an emergency exit back there. When I worked in this library during college, my co-workers always kept it propped open so that they could use the exit to sneak out for a smoke.

⁓⤳⧽⧼⤲⁓

As we ran down the hall, I glanced back and could see that a couple dozen zombies were already at the glass door through which we had just passed. And one of them was Gabe.

The dead would get through that door at any moment, so there was no time to waste. Still pulling Tempest along after me, I swerved right, then left, then right, and then flung open the exit door.

⁓⤳⧽⧼⤲⁓

Our escape from the library had only bought us a momentary reprieve. The herd would track us down again in short order. We couldn't breathe with complete ease for even a brief moment because there were a few stragglers still milling about aimlessly outside the library.

"This way!" Tempest said, gesturing toward

the liberal arts building.

"No, this way, Tempest. I came in the Hummer. We need to reach it." I pointed toward the parking lot near the student union.

We started to run for it but quickly began to attract unwanted attention. Coming to a stop in the middle of an open quad, we could see that, in every direction, there were three or four zombies expressing visible interest in the two of us.

"Ugh." Tempest said.

I had to agree. Looking toward the library, I could see that zombies were also starting to reemerge from its front facade. This was bad.

"Run for the university center." I instructed Tempest. I pointed to make sure she knew where I was indicating. She nodded, and then I made a break for it.

It was like playing dodge-ball with zombies. Thank goodness for their poor motor skills and general lack of coordination. Half of them fell over when they tried to lunge for us. I zigzagged forward toward the student union, ducking out of the way of each lumbering zombie as it began to get close. From what I could tell, Tempest was doing the same.

By the time I reached the nearest side of the building, there was a wall of the dead amassing behind us. There were just too many of them. Hundreds upon hundreds, milling about, looking rank and hungry.

Catching up to me, Tempest stopped, panting, and said, "There's no way we'll make it to the parking lot right now. We'll just have to play dead."

I looked at her incredulously.

"What, just drop to the ground and go limp?" I asked.

Tempest gave a half-chuckle. "Hardly." she said. "The zombies would catch our scent in no time."

"So, what then?"

"Come here." she instructed. She ran for the broken glass facade of the campus bookstore located at the corner of the student union,. I could see from the carnage that a violent struggle had taken place here. Stepping over jagged glass, Tempest entered and immediately began moving pieces of the slimy corpses, gathering them into a pile.

"Our scent will be camouflaged if we hide

amidst the bodies." she explained.

I nodded. "That smell would camouflage anything." I agreed.

The zombies were rapidly getting closer and would reach us soon, so we lay down and covered ourselves with the dead.

The zombies were soon all around us.

I knew that I should just keep my damned eyes shut, but I couldn't do it. I was looking straight into the face of a corpse that hadn't been alive for some time now. The top quarter of its head was completely missing; in all likelihood it had been shot off. His ears appeared to have mummified. They were shriveled, dry and black. I was sure that if I had reached up and clasped them in my hands, they would have just crumbled away like burnt paper. It seemed strange to me that the ears could be so desiccated when the face was so horribly moist. The eyes had liquefied long ago, yet the sockets still appeared to be goopy and dribbling. Putrefied skin hung from what remained of its forehead and also from along its jaw, dangling there in thin, wet sheets. Slimy, receding lips curled away from the black hole that had once been a mouth; hanging ever so slightly open, it provided me with an unwelcome glimpse into the disease, unspeakable rot, and filth festering within the body. I had to remind himself that this body had once been a human being. The worst part, though, was that my eyes kept fixating on the maggots that were happily worming their way in and out of the rancid flesh of its cheeks.

I stifled a gag, desperately trying to remain quiet as I did so. My stomach was churning. Finally, I had to force myself to shut my eyes. If I threw up, the zombie horde would be on me within moments and would completely tear me apart. I would be completely devoured. They would gnaw on my bones.

My fear was overwhelming, and the smell was unbearable. God, why couldn't my body have mercy on me and just let me pass out?

The sound of shuffling was all around me. The herd must be passing directly around the piles of bodies beneath which Tempest and I were hidden. I shuddered involuntarily and then prayed that none of the undead had perceived the motion.

I was biding my time and trying not to breath. I hoped that Nathan wouldn't inadvertently shift or sneeze or anything else to give us away.

The worst part about my situation was that the mound of bodies I had buried myself under had shifted, and now I had decomposing genitals dangling in my face.

Eventually, the noises around us died away. Unfortunately, so did the light.

"Nathan?" I whispered.

"Nathan?" I hissed again. Please, oh, please, could he just hear me? I didn't want to have to speak any louder.

Then I heard a muffled "Mmmffph."

"I think this is probably our best chance to try to run for your car."

"Mmmgkk" he responded.

The bodies began to shift as he slowly pushed them off of him. I began to do the same.

Nathan wiped his mouth roughly against his shoulder and then whispered "If I had opened my mouth, something very nasty would have fallen in."

I nodded, indicating that I completely understood.

We were both so covered in corpse muck that, if we had moved slowly and stiltedly, we probably could have walked right up to a group of zombies and passed for one of their own. We didn't test that though.

It was night now, and I couldn't see very well, but I kept close to Nathan as we ran for his vehicle.

Although no longer as tightly packed, the herd was still ambling around the area. Several of them took notice of our movement and began to lumber toward us, but we easily made it to the parking lot ahead of them. We got in and tore out of there.

Chapter 12 - Things Could Be Worse

We were headed for Nathan's place, which was fine with me. I just wanted to change out of my clothes, which were plastered to me with corpse seepage.

As Nathan shifted, a pained look spread across his face. Then I noticed that there was blood on his shirt. Which was torn.

Shit. He was hurt.

"You're injured." I said. "Let me see it."

Nathan winced as he lifted his shirt but said nothing. He had cut himself on broken glass. Around the main laceration, there were smaller abrasions in which tiny fragments of glass were still embedded. I breathed a private sigh of relief. He would be okay. It didn't look as though he had injured anything vital, but the cut was pretty deep, and I bet it hurt like hell.

"It's not bad. I can dress it." I said.

Nathan nodded, going rigid as he tried to hide his pain when I touched around the wound.

"You know, suffering stoically is incredibly sexy."

"I'm glad it's good for something." he said. Then he asked me, "Tempest?"

"Yes?"

"What's your real name?"

"That doesn't matter." I answered.

"Well, that sucked." Tempest offered conversationally as we got out of the Hummer.

"It did. It did indeed." I replied. I unlocked the door to my house, and we stepped in together.

We showered (separately, of course) and changed clothes. I gave Tempest a pair of my sweatpants and a t-shirt and then changed into similar attire myself. She cleaned and dressed my wound.

I was planning to give Tempest my bed for

the night and take the sofa. In the morning, I could take her home or wherever she liked, or she could stay, if she so chose.

She followed me into my bedroom when I went to change the sheets and set out fresh candles, but stopped first and glanced at Mother's door.

"You don't want to go in there."

"Is that where you kept her?"

"Yes. I've tried to clean it up, but it still reeks..."

No matter how much I clean, the walls are still stained and caked with textured filth.

Looking at the door somehow as if I'd seen it for the first time, I added "I'm ashamed that I lived that way for so long. " I surprised myself with my own candor.

"We're all ashamed of things we have done. Just let it go."

Then Tempest came into my bedroom and put her arms around me.

We both had a lot of pent up emotions to vent. I won't kiss and tell. All I'll say is that our evening suddenly got a whole hell of a lot better.

———————

We fucked each other's brains out. Oh, come on, did you expect us to just blush and hold hands forever? We're adults, and there is no tomorrow. We sure as hell are going to live for today.

The first kiss was gentle. Nathan leaned down and softly kissed my upper lip, then my lower one, then ran his tongue just lightly between them. Those first kisses were fluttering. Then we kissed deeply, our tongues passionately twisting and turning tumultuously, like two ravenous serpents, as they intertwined.

I threw myself into it. God only knows I needed something to throw myself into. And desire is like intoxication; it allows you to let go and forget everything else.

I practically tore Nathan's clothes off of him. He was slim but defined, and I wanted to run my mouth over every inch of him. I had to remember to be careful of the wound on his chest, limiting my nail raking to other areas of his body.

I kissed Nathan's ears, his neck, his chest. I

was ravenous for our love-making, and when he started to lick and kiss my nipples, it was more than I could stand. My hands could not get his pants off fast enough.

"Do you have a condom?" I breathed.

"What?" Nathan said, looking startled and confused. He sat up in bed. "No, of course I don't have a condom. Why the hell would I have a condom? I've been living alone with my dead mother for years..."

"OK, point taken, relax." I said. "Let's not spoil the mood."

I grabbed him by his shirt collar and pulled him back down to me, kissing him passionately.

I don't want to get pregnant. But fuck it. In this fucked up world we live in, I sure as hell wasn't going to give up this rare moment of joy and pleasure. Besides, condoms stopped being produced when the outbreak started, so they'd probably all be expired by now anyway. Maybe I can get some birth control pills through one of the runners I know. I have a huge stash of valuable items to trade.

It would be tacky to talk about his cock, right? Oh, fuck it. It was glorious. Big, fat, and glorious. And when he first thrust into me, I couldn't believe how incredible it felt. How could I have forgotten in these past few years how fucking good fucking felt? Or had it ever actually felt *this* good before? I don't think so. We made love with the passionate desperation of people who did not know if they would have a tomorrow. At least the apocalypse has turned out to be good for something.

Afterwards, we both collapsed, physically spent. Then we gently touched each other in silence for a while, just running our fingertips over each other's body, learning every square inch.

The way I see it, the world ended four years ago. It's just some kind of cruel joke that we're still here, pointlessly trying to keep ourselves alive. What for? Some hard-wired survival instinct built into our genetic code that tells us to perpetuate the species. It's outdated, outmoded, obsolete.

But there has never been any point beyond the one that we make for ourselves, and that hasn't changed. Existence is as meaningful or meaningless as we dictate it to be. We enrich our lives, making them worthwhile and imbuing them with personal meaning through our experiences. Or, conversely, we diminish life, detracting from its potential and devaluing it by choosing to accept dismal surroundings, mental fatigue, and emotional death.

"What are you thinking about?" Nathan asked.

"Isn't that supposed to be the girl's line?" I said, smirking. "I was just thinking that things change on a dime. You can be in perfect health one day, then get a scratch on your pinky toe. It gets inexplicably infected and, two weeks later, you've gone septic and dropped dead. That's the way it goes—the nature of life. So you sure as hell better try to enjoy things while you can."

"Hedonist."

"Hell, yeah. Of course I am. What would be the point of restraint and self-denial? It's the only way of living that makes any sense."

"Mmmm... I see." Nathan said.

And then we fucked again.

Later that night, curled in bed together, Tempest and I continued our pillow talk.

I was feeling unusually optimistic. "Do you think we can wait them out?" I asked her. "Decomposition has already immobilized a lot of them. Eventually you've got to figure that the zombie threat will die on its own. They'll rot away."

"But there will always be more dead. The thing that reanimates human flesh is in all of us. We're them. It's just a matter of time. I could drop dead peacefully from a heart attack in the night, and the next thing you know you'd be waking up to me eating your face. There's no getting away from that."

"No, but the mother lode of the dead have already degraded. There aren't enough living anymore to create the massive hordes of undead we saw when the infection first presented itself. Even that group of them at the university won't be able to walk around much longer. The streets are pretty much clear already. Most of that first wave of original living dead are now little more than pieces of bodies that quiver in place or drag themselves along, slug-like. They don't exactly pose a threat anymore."

"Hmmm." she said, considering it. "Well, maybe." She paused, then asked, "Nathan?"

"Mmhmm?" cradling her in my arms.

"My name was Hope."

"What?"

"My name. Before. It was Hope."

"Really?"

"Yeah." she said in her most deadpan voice.

"Wow."

"I know. It seemed painfully ironic. That's why I stopped using it. I felt like I was being mocked by my own name."

"Does it necessarily have to be ridiculously naive to have a glimmer of hope?"

"It sure seemed like it for a long time. I don't know, maybe it doesn't have to be. I'm open to being wrong. I'd sure like to be."

I squeezed her tight. "You know, when we're old, we'll have to sleep apart in locked rooms." I said.

"Or we could just choose to continue enjoying our lives and live dangerously, accepting joining the ranks of the undead together." she said, a smile playing at the corners of her mouth.

"How romantic." I said, and I meant it. That sounded pretty fabulous at the moment.

She smiled. It lit up her face, and I couldn't resist leaning in to kiss her.

That morning, I woke before Tempest did. I went into the bathroom to change the bandage on my chest, but I must have made some noise, because I woke her. When Tempest came into the bathroom, for a moment I was worried that things would be different with the new day. I was afraid that the exceptional closeness we felt for one another last night would have passed away. But she just took the bandage from me and dressed my wound.

Afterwards, I neatly folded the old bandage up and put it in the cabinet.

"What are you doing?"

"Saving it. It's from our first night together."

"You're hopelessly sentimental, aren't you?"

"I do have a nostalgic streak..."

"Good, you can be in charge of keeping up the family albums for us." she said.

I pulled her to me right there standing over the toilet, and we exchanged a prolonged kiss. After that, we went back into the bedroom. For several hours.

Dangers are certainly still rampant in this world, but we are starting to find moments of joy in spite of the world around us. Making existence worth experiencing is the most we can hope for, even in the best of circumstances. Under these post-apocalyptic conditions, we're definitely making the best of things.

— Nathan & Tempest

Excerpt from
Flesh Eaters

Chapter 1

A s I AWOKE, I hazily noticed that my face was pressed against hard, cool cement. It wasn't gravelly sidewalk cement, but vaguely shiny, almost lacquered cement like one commonly finds in college dormitories and other clinical institutions. Although I wasn't accustomed to waking up on hard surfaces, I was willing to ignore it for the moment and flutter in and out of consciousness for a while. Unfortunately, I wasn't allowed the luxury of easing into consciousness, as I like to do after sleeping, for, as my eyes focused, I was compelled to jolt up.

I was immediately, painfully, alert; a large, muscular man was standing over me. I couldn't help thinking about how closely he resembled the brutish archetype I'd seen in so many video games. His chest was disproportionately large, and his bulbous arms sprouted out of his faded T-shirt, contributing to his polygonal appearance. His hands were oversized, even for his frame,

154

and looked blocky. His taut, angular face stared down at me.

The large man hovering over me was aiming what appeared to be an equally large revolver at my head. I focused my attention there, staring into the depths of the barrel, bewildered. He was saying something, but my adrenaline was pumping, and the sound of my heart was deafening. Aware that this was a classic "fight or flight" situation, I bitterly began to wonder what was keeping me from choosing a response. I seemed frozen, or perhaps time had stood still.

There was someone else, behind him, shouting; this figure was a blur to me—a blue blur (his shirt, I think) with a shiny, metallic tracer. The blur's words "Shoot her! Shoot her!" seemed to make their way through the cyclone of movement and confusion.

My trance was broken. Facing the absurd realization that my death was imminent, I sprang awake. I frantically looked around me, desperate for something, anything. A nearby exit caught my attention; a few yards from me, there was a dark hole at the bottom of the wall. The hole was close to two feet tall and appeared either to be an air vent or, perhaps, my reeling mind postulated, a drainage duct leading to sewers. I began to start for it, but jerked myself to a stop before I had even begun to move, quickly seeing that it was futile. The hole was blocked off; across the opening hung what looked like it would prove to be a very heavy latticed, metal grate.

I started to turn away in search of some other means of escape, but caught a glimpse of something odd from the corner of my eye. Looking again, I noticed that a handgun sat near the grate. There was a shotgun a few feet beyond that.

I didn't stop to look a gift gun in the mouth. Somewhere deep in the recesses of my churning psyche, I was whispering reassuringly to myself. In a soothing voice, I told myself that I didn't need to (or have time to) question why I had woken up in this strange, new environ, let alone why there was a stockpile of guns lying a few yards from me. I tried to reach for the handgun, but my progress was impeded.

To this day, I still can't work out all of the details of those first few minutes after I woke up; everything was happening too fast. My adversaries' shouting mixed with my own, bleeding together into a thunderous, unintelligible hum. Their movements seemed to meld them into one giant, nebulous enemy. Straining for the revolver, I felt as though I were fumbling for a light switch in the dark. I remember thinking that my burly assailant must be sitting on my chest; I'm still not sure if he was, or if my lower half had failed to wake up with the rest of me. Whatever was holding me back, I lay prone and, stretching and contorting, finally managed to wriggle away from the two men, just far enough to grasp the gun.

I had no idea if the thing was loaded, but since I'd heard a hammer being cocked amidst the cacophony, I knew it was my only hope. The blue blur was rushing at me, looking more and more like a skinny, unkempt man with a gun as he did so. I raised the gun and fired.

I am not a gun person. I have had no formal training with guns. In fact, the only time my father took me shooting, the sound of the guns firing made me cover my ears with my hands and cry to be taken home. I would have been lucky to hit my blurry blue attacker at all. That I shot him in the forehead with what to a casual observer would have only looked like dead accuracy is another baffling detail in the bizarre, surrealistic world I had fallen into.

I had no time to breathe a sigh of relief, as the second gunman was bearing down on me, uttering nasty guttural noises. That he hadn't shot me yet was inexplicable to me at the time. In retrospect, I attribute it to the crazed way I had been shaking my head around. Since I had not actually faced a situation remotely like this before, it seemed perfectly appropriate to me to hysterically thrash my head about. I believe my spasmodic behavior saved my life. I'm sure he was holding out for a clean shot; he needed to conserve ammo.

I managed to stagger to my feet. He was only a foot or two away from me now and was trying to grab my arms, to hold me still.

I raised the gun toward him, levying it to what I presumed was his chest level. I wasn't even looking at what I was doing. I could only look at him—and his gun. His gun was shiny and black, and I would have sworn it was the size of a cannon. He was still trying to get a good hold on me, to get a clear shot at my head.

I fired. He staggered back; a blood spot materialized on the upper chest area of his shirt, instantly plastering the cloth to his chest, and began to spread outwards. He swayed and then lumbered forward for me again. I shot him again. I didn't even hear the gun shots as I unloaded them. I knew I'd fired when he fell backwards. His heavy frame hit the floor solidly, resonating. Blood emptied out of him and pooled around his body.

The echo of his fall began to fade, and was replaced with momentary stillness. I stood up and inhaled deeply.

Then the bullet-ridden oaf leaped up and lunged at me. His eyes were milky and dead.

I was vaguely aware that my feet had involuntarily begun to shuffle backwards; I remember hearing the soles of my boots scuffing against the cement below me.

I felt as though I'd walked into a zombie movie. The reassuring whisper that resided inside of me promptly gave up and went silent. Still, I had no time to be incredulous; he had hold of me. I accepted that I was living in an obscure, low-budget movie and resolved to deal with my complete and utter loss of sanity after I had disposed of my undead assailant. He had dropped his gun after the second shot I fired into him. It lay in his blood, forgotten. This hulking abomination was more concerned with immediate gratification now. He was looming over me, grabbing at my arms, digging his nails into me. His mouth was descending toward my shoulder, gaping hungrily.

Face to face with what bore more than a passing resemblance to a hungry zombie, I did what any self-respecting horror buff would. I shot for the head. At point blank range, he really didn't have a chance.

The monstrosity roared and seemed to fall back in slow motion. His limbs twitched wildly. Then everything went silent.

Dumbstruck, I stood, motionless, staring down at his body. Anyone who's ever seen a horror flick knows you should never stand within arm's reach of your fallen adversary. But I lingered there, inches from him. For hours? For days? Maybe it was only minutes. All sense of time deserted me that day (nor have I ever fully regained it since).

The bullet wound in his head couldn't have been more than a dime in size; it was deep and dark, but bloodless. The skin around the wound was loose and pushed into unnatural ridges. Staring blankly down at the carcass, I found myself thinking that his forehead resembled a mountain range with the abscess, a valley in its middle. Then I began to think that his forehead looked more like an enormous shortbread cookie with a dollop of dark raspberry filling at its center. This analogy disturbed me, and I forced myself to look away.

I surveyed the room. It was small, dimly lit with covered, fluorescent lighting, and made of cement, painted off-white. Just beyond the corpse, there was a drain in the middle of the slightly concave cement floor.

The drain was currently being put to work; a stream of blood was winding a meandering path into it, emptying in a slow but steady drip. My assailant had recklessly trekked his own vital fluids around him, daubing the floor with his juices during his repeated, frantic attempts to assault me. In addition to the substantial puddle he had left near the middle of the room, streaks and droplets blanketed the chamber.

The grated hole and shotgun lay behind me to my left. I began to think about what chance I might have of ever wrenching the damned grate off and where the opening might lead. I was not hopeful on either count. The more frail of my two antagonists lay near this duct. Taking a few steps closer, I was able to get a better look at him.

He was lying face up. The bullet wound was hard to miss. If the wound in his forehead was larger than his friend's, it was imperceptibly so. However, long trails of blood had run, in rivulets, down all sides of his face, pooling around his chin and in his ears. Avoiding looking at his eyes, I gingerly grasped a tuft of his ratty hair and lifted his head. The back half of his skull was almost entirely gone. His head looked like a broken hard-boiled egg out of which someone had plucked the yolk. Then I began to notice the bits of gore strewn about him that were presumably scraps of brain matter.

Abruptly dropping his head, I stifled a gag and turned back around.

Where the hell was I?

Turning, I looked to my right. The room in

which I found myself appeared to be a very large shower room. This hypothesis was strongly corroborated by the fact that there was an ornate-looking shower head on the opposite wall. There was also a door—a fairly standard, run-of-the-mill opaque glass door. How could I have missed it before? Feeling suddenly decidedly less restrained, I walked over to it. My boots made unpleasant squishing noises in the wetness below me.

The door was slightly ajar; bright light poured through the crack. I cautiously peered into the adjoining room. It was a bathroom. More importantly, it appeared to be empty. I slid the door open.

The bathroom was immaculate. It was brilliantly white: the walls were ivory with alabaster molding, and the sink faucet and porcelain commode gleamed. The mirror above the sink reflected the overhead light, making the room's illumination almost blinding. It looked totally unlived in; there was no rug on the floor, no toothbrush on the sink counter—not a single sign of use. It looked like a mock-up bathroom in a department store.

I entered the virginal room, tracking blood across the floor as I went. Stopping in front of the mirror, I ventured a look at myself. My left cheek was streaked with blood. My hair was knotted and caked with foul stickiness; strands clung to my face. I was wearing an army-green T-shirt, spackled with blood, and loose-fitting grey-black jeans, which also bore some nasty, darker smears. I had had some vain hope that seeing what I was wearing would jog my memory. I thought I might remember where I had been when I put my clothes on, or what I had been doing—some event that might have led me here. No memory came. They were my clothes, but they offered me no recollection of how I had gotten here.

I set the gun down on the sink counter and washed my face. After spending a few moments fruitlessly trying to pick coagulated blood from my matted hair, I gave up in disgust. Even though the room gave off the impression that no human had ever set foot in it before, I figured that I had best search it, just to be thorough. I didn't want to miss even the smallest clue that might lend me a wisp of insight into where I was or what was going on. Besides, I'd played enough Resident Evil to know that, during a zombie outbreak, protagonists were supposed to pilfer any supplies they could find. I rifled through the drawers below the counter. The first drawer produced a bottle containing two aspirin, an empty tube of toothpaste, and a pen cap. I pocketed the aspirin. The second drawer appeared empty, but careful examination led to what I considered an exciting discovery. In the back corner lay a small, brown band—a hair tie.

Shutting the drawers, I quickly gathered up my fetid hair and bound it into a ponytail. Feeling moderately refreshed, I retrieved the gun from the counter and turned to the door on my right—the door that led out into the rest of the apartment, if where I found myself was indeed an apartment

Excerpt from Daydreams
of Seppuku

In the late 1990s, law enforcement officials estimated that there were as many as five serial killers active in the New Orleans area.

None were ever caught.

Chapter 1

July 12, 1999
2:06 p.m.

Behind the boarded up windows at 1622 Wellsworth, the semi-conscious figure twisted her bound limbs futilely. She tried to cry out, but only small, muffled sounds could escape from behind the wadded-up, grease-stained rag that was stuffed deep into her mouth. The television across from her blared; it could have easily drowned out much louder noises than those of which this girl was currently capable.

Ursula, a nineteen-year-old street urchin, was bleached white-blonde and adorned with piercings, tattoos, and tread-marks, to which she had recently acquired new, more grim scarifications to add to her motley ensemble. A long, jagged cut ran across her left brow, giving her the appearance of a freshly mauled boxer. It had bled down into her eye while she was unconscious, and the eye was now crusted shut. Welts and scratches littered her wrists near the ligatures that bound them. The tendon behind her left knee had been cleanly severed.

She ached all over.

How had she gotten here? What had happened to her? Ursula knew that she had been partying in the Quarter, but after that, there were only random blurry images in place of any solid memory.

The young woman continued to writhe, twisting and contorting her torso and half-numb, effectively vestigial, limbs in a feeble attempt to see her surroundings. She was lying on a stained cot facing a smudged, once-white wall. The light of the television flickered across her back, casting grotesque shadows, like ghostly finger puppets, across the wall in front of her.

In the distance, she could hear someone opening the front door, his keys jingling.

Her one functional eye grew wide with fear, and she began to struggle frantically, but with no effect.

The footsteps were inside now, approaching. From behind her, the doorknob, whining, turned, and the door swung open into the room.

Excerpt from Death:
the Travelogues

Prologue

The nice thing about death is that it makes all of your problems inconsequential. However, this is primarily because, typically, death means the end of consciousness, and all of the needling little inconveniences that come along with it – obligations, embarrassments, worries over trivial matters...

I seem to have been part of some tiny cosmic glitch – a miniscule hole in the fabric of existence, or maybe a just a hiccup, one random number out of place in the gigantic computer program of life.

I died, but my consciousness failed to turn off. This was rather unpleasant until I figured out that I didn't need my physical body. Being a consciousness trapped in a rotting husk of meat is rather disconcerting. The living are so accustomed to the organic transports that carry them around that they often cannot separate their concepts of self from their own bodies. I was guilty of similar ignorance. It did not occur to me that my body and I were no longer tethered together. I languished in my own putrid, wrecked remains for well over a week before I figured out that I could just get out and walk.

I imagine that you are wondering then, do I have no physical form? Well, yes, and no. Bodies are merely vehicles for transporting people's consciousnesses around. So, I occasionally hitch a ride.

"Possession" is an ugly word; it is laden with negative associations. There is no malice inherent in what I do; I'm just catching a lift. Sometimes I sit in the back seat and enjoy the scenery. Sometimes I drive.

To brazenly mix metaphors, imagine that you ate the same meal every day of your life. Maybe it is a good meal, or maybe it is an unpalatable one. Regardless, it is always the same one. If you suddenly had a chance to try every conceivable dish currently prepared on the planet, wouldn't you jump at the chance? Well, I would.

A single life is myopic; only since death, with a smorgasbord of bodies available to inhabit, have I begun to form a vague conception of human existence.

Bodies are so... limiting. Being confined to one body, imprisoned in a single ambulatory shell, is so depressingly narrow an existence that it makes me feel claustrophobic to even contemplate it. I can't fathom how I ever was able to stand it. No wonder I was unhappy; no wonder, essentially, at least deep down, all living people are.

I want it to be clear that I am not a ghost or a spirit. If my spirit did survive death, I'm sure it's contentedly floating around a forest somewhere, suffusing with nature. Whatever it is doing, if it exists, has nothing to do with me. I was once a person, but now I am merely a consciousness, or simply an entity. What I was in life doesn't matter; I was the sum of my limited experiences. But, still, my aim is not to be unsettling, and the living tend to find comfort in familiarity, so I suppose I should make an attempt to have you "get to know me." I'll start from the beginning.

About the Author

Alisha Adkins is a native of New Orleans and has also lived in Dallas, San Francisco, and Nagasaki Prefecture, Japan. She holds a Masters degree in education from the University of New Orleans and worked as a high school teacher for ten years before eventually escaping. She currently works as an educational consultant for a major publishing company.

Alisha Adkins is the author of *Flesh Eaters*, *Daydreams of Seppuku*, and *Death: the Travelogues*.

www.ingramcontent.com/pod-product-compliance
Lightning Source LLC
Chambersburg PA
CBHW071242130626
46556CB00003B/1120